TWELVE HOURS
OF TEMPTATION

set
to stop
his,' he

TWELVE HOURS OF TEMPTATION

BY

SHOMA NARAYANAN

First published in Great Britain 2014
by Mills & Boon, an imprint of Harlequin (UK) Limited,
Large Print edition 2014
Eton House, 18-24 Paradise Road,
Richmond, Surrey, TW9 1SR

© 2014 Shoma Narayanan

ISBN: 978-0-263-24102-0

Harlequin (UK) Limited's policy is to use papers that
are natural, renewable and recyclable products and made
from wood grown in sustainable forests. The logging
and manufacturing processes conform to the legal
environmental regulations of the country of origin.

Printed and bound in Great Britain
by CPI Antony Rowe, Chippenham, Wiltshire

To Badri

CHAPTER ONE

'BRIAN'S SELLING THE AGENCY.'

The words didn't sink in at first because Melissa was busy squinting at her keyboard. Damn the *O* key. It was jamming up again. The last line she'd typed read as if it had a particularly nasty swear word in it—the difference a single missing *o* could make was amazing.

'I need a new keyboard,' she said. 'Unless… *What* did you say?'

Pleased at the impact she'd created, Neera plopped her lush backside onto Melissa's desk and beamed at her pretty young friend. 'It's true. He's going to announce it today.'

Melissa stared at her in dismay. Brian Mendonca had set up the tiny advertising agency thirty years ago, and it was more like an extended family than a workplace. Melissa herself had been working there for a little over two years, and she loved the place.

'Who's buying it?'

'Maximus Advertising. They're expanding… and Brian wants to retire and go back to Goa, apparently.' Neera looked over her shoulder and then leaned down. 'Don't look now, but the guy who's taking over is with Brian right now. He's pretty hot, actually, can't be very old…'

As Melissa instinctively turned, Neera tugged her back, and all she caught a glimpse of was a tall man walking out of the main entrance of the office with Brian.

'His name's Samir Razdan,' Neera reported two days later.

Melissa abandoned the ad she was working on to search the internet for the name.

'Impressive,' she said. 'Studied in the US. He's been working for only ten years and he's already Maximus's corporate strategy head. Looks pretty arrogant, though—like he thinks he's a lot smarter than anyone else.'

The picture on the Maximus website showed a strong-featured man in his early thirties—even the grim expression in his eyes didn't detract from his good looks.

'Shh...' Neera muttered, and Melissa turned to see Brian bearing down on them with the subject of the photograph in tow.

The man was magnificent in real life. There was no other word for it, Melissa thought as she stared at him. Well over six feet in height, he towered over Brian—and the contrast between Brian's rather pudgy middle-aged form and Samir Razdan's perfectly proportioned physique was striking.

She hadn't had enough time to switch screens, and her browser still had the Maximus website open. Melissa wondered if he'd overheard her remark.

'Meet some of the most talented people on the team,' Brian said, beaming at both of them. 'Neera is our creative head, and Melissa's our star copywriter.'

'It's so nice to meet you,' Neera gushed, holding out her hand.

Samir took it after a second's hesitation and said, 'It's a pleasure.'

His tone was formal, almost dismissive, and Melissa immediately felt her hackles rise. Neera could come across as a bit silly at times, but she was brilliant at her work and Samir had absolutely no business looking down at her.

'And this is Melissa,' Brian said fondly, and his expression suggested an indulgent grandfather introducing a favourite but slightly unpredictable grandchild.

'Hi,' Melissa said coolly, giving Samir a slow once-over. She didn't stand up—even in her two-inch heels she would probably only reach his chin. And Brian hadn't *said* that Samir was taking over the company—there was no need for her to spring to attention.

As her eyes drifted over his body she couldn't help noticing how broad his shoulders were, and how perfectly his formal blue shirt and grey trousers fitted his athletic frame…. For a few seconds she actually felt her breathing get a bit out of control. Then she gave herself a mental slap. Getting distracted was *not* supposed to happen. The 'once-over technique' was something her sister-in-law had taught her. Used to ogling women themselves, most men were made profoundly uncomfortable by an attractive woman looking them over as if she found something lacking.

Okay, so that was *most* men. When her eyes met Samir's again he didn't look the least bit fazed—if anything, there was the merest hint of a twinkle in his eyes.

'Your star copywriter, you say?' he said to Brian.

'Yes, one of her ads has been nominated for an award this year,' Brian said. Clearly eager to undo the damage his protégée was hell-bent on doing, he went on, 'I'm expecting it to win silver at the very least—if not gold.'

'Impressive,' Samir said, and Melissa had no way of knowing if he was being sarcastic or not. 'Well, I'll see you ladies around.'

His eyes flickered for a second towards Melissa's computer screen. The Maximus website was still open, with Samir Razdan's picture occupying pride of place at the top right-hand corner. The man himself didn't react, however, giving the girls a polite nod and continuing towards the exit.

'He seems pretty nice,' Neera said as the doors closed behind him.

Melissa stared at her in disbelief. 'You can't be serious!' she said, turning to the elderly Hindi copywriter who sat next to her. 'You saw him, Dubeyji, what did you think?'

'He's a good businessman,' Dubeyji said a little sadly. 'Doesn't let people know what he's thinking. But I'm sure he'll get rid of the old fogeys like me. I know how Maximus runs—it's like a factory. We'll just be a little insignificant part of their operations. They wouldn't even have looked at us if it wasn't for the awards we've got recently.'

'He's right,' Melissa burst out, getting to her feet in agitation. 'It's not about this Razdan guy. Maximus will probably sack half of us, and the rest will have to go work in one of those hideous blue glass buildings and wear access cards and queue up for lunch at the cafeteria...'

'And hopefully we'll get paid every month,' said Devdeep, the agency's client servicing head, as he strolled up. 'Melissa, we all love Brian, but creative freedom is a bit of a luxury when we're losing clients every day.'

'He's great at what he does,' Melissa said hotly. 'None of us have one tenth of his talent and—'

'I agree,' Devdeep said. 'The point is the world's moved a little beyond print advertising. I know TV might be a bit much for an agency this size to handle, though we could have done it if we'd expanded at the right time. But there's digital advertising and social media—let's admit it: we've lost some of our best clients because Brian doesn't hold with "all that new technology rubbish".'

'He's right,' Neera said. 'Melly, if Brian continues to run this place we'll all be out of jobs within a year. Awards or no awards. He's a bit of a...well, not a dinosaur, exactly, but definitely ancient.'

'A mastodon, maybe,' Devdeep said, giving Melissa an irritatingly superior smile. 'Or a woolly mammoth.'

'Remind me not to ask you guys to bat for me *ever*,' Melissa muttered, and turned back to her computer to pound savagely at the keys.

She was unswervingly loyal to Brian, and she didn't understand how everyone else wasn't the same. Brian had done so much for each of them—Melissa knew that he'd given Devdeep a job when he'd been sacked from another agency, and that he'd advanced Neera a pot of money to pay for her mum's bypass surgery a year ago. Their criticising him was a bit like a bunch of Kolkata street kids saying that the Sisters of Charity could do with a make-over and a new uniform.

'I thought you hadn't yet told your staff about the buy-out?' said Samir.

'I haven't,' Brian replied. 'But it's a small office—the finance guys guessed something was happening and the word must have spread.'

'Evidently,' Samir agreed, his voice dry. 'I'd suggest you talk to them. Those women were looking a bit jittery.'

Or at least one woman had been—the other had been anything but. For a few seconds his mind dwelled on the coolly challenging way in which she'd spoken to him. She'd known who he was, and it hadn't fazed her in the least.

As it turned out Brian didn't have to speak to the team as Devdeep had called everyone into a room and was in the process of giving them a pep talk. Brian didn't object—he was already looking forward to a life of retirement, and anyway, Devdeep would be managing the bulk of the agency work until the sale went through.

Samir Razdan was a corporate restructuring expert, not an adman—there was even a chance Devdeep would get to head the agency once Samir got it fully integrated into the Maximus empire.

'It's all very well for you,' Melissa told Brian crossly as he dropped her at her hostel in Colaba that evening. 'You and Aunty Liz will have the time of your lives, going off on cruises and world tours, while all of us slog away for Robot Samir.'

Brian gave her a quizzical look. 'You met him for all of five minutes,' he pointed out. 'Surely that's not long enough to start calling him names?'

'I looked him up before that,' she said. 'He's a businessman through and through. I don't think he has a creative bone in his body. He won't do the agency any good, Brian, he'll only try and squeeze out the last possible rupee of revenue he can. And you can tell a lot in five minutes—he's pretty cold-blooded, and he obviously thinks he's God's gift to womankind.'

'Ah...' Brian said. 'So that's it. Paid more attention to Neera, did he?'

Brian was in his mid-fifties, and he still admired the fair-skinned, luscious beauties of his youth—Neera was a pretty fine example of the type.

'*No,*' Melissa said, exasperated. Apart from trivialising her concerns about the takeover, it wasn't even true. Samir had hardly noticed Neera, and while he might not have been bowled over by Melissa she'd at least caught his attention.

Unbidden, her thoughts drifted back to the second their eyes had met…then she shook herself angrily. Brian's habit of reducing everything to a simple man-woman equation was as annoying as it was infectious.

'Look, I'm sorry I took off at you,' she said. 'It's just that you and Aunty Liz have been like family to me, and I don't know… I'm just a bit…'

The car had stopped outside the working women's hostel where Melissa lived, and Brian reached out to give her a clumsy pat on the shoulder.

'Sorry,' Melissa said again, taking in his anxious expression. 'Don't worry, I'm not about to start howling. Just…stay in touch, OK? Even when you're off living the high life,' she added as she climbed out of the car, smiling at him before she closed the door.

'Yes, of course.'

Overall, Brian looked rather relieved to be rid of her, and she couldn't blame him. Emotional scenes weren't really his thing.

'I'll ask Liz to call you. Fix dinner with us this Sunday, maybe, and we can talk things over.'

He was about to drive off when something struck him and he rolled the window down. 'Don't judge Samir too hastily, OK? He's a great guy—just a little reserved. Wait till you get to know him better.'

Melissa waited while he drove off and then walked into the hostel, uncharacteristic tears pricking at her eyelids. She was distantly related to Brian's wife, and two years ago, when her family had turned against her, Liz and Brian had brought her to Mumbai, given her a job and helped her settle down. Brian insisted that she'd more than repaid the debt with the amount of hard work she'd put in since joining the agency, but she felt more grateful and connected to the couple than she had to anyone else in her life. Brian's announcement had come as a shock—it felt as if her last source of emotional support was now gone.

* * *

Three weeks later, when Samir moved into the Mendonca Advertising corner office, he found himself automatically looking for the dusky elfin woman he'd met the first day he'd visited the office. Brian had spoken to him about her later, and he was intrigued by the few things that Brian had let drop. He didn't see her for the first week, though, and it was only at the beginning of the next week that he thought to ask someone where she was.

'Is everyone in the office, Devdeep?' he asked.

Devdeep wrinkled his forehead. 'Yes, I think so,' he said. 'Was there someone you'd like to meet in particular? Because I've already lined up discussions with the team heads, but I can rejig them if needed.'

Distracted for a second by a vivid mental image of jigging team heads, Samir shook his head. 'No. There were a couple of women Brian introduced me to the first day I was here. I can't see either of them around.'

'Ah, Neera and Melissa,' Devdeep said. 'Neera's

not well, but Melissa should be around—actually, she should be here already. I'll speak to her about it. She's normally never late.'

Samir heroically resisted the impulse to tell Devdeep not to get his panties in a twist and said instead, 'Don't worry about it. I was just wondering if she was on leave today.'

Ten minutes later he was left in no doubt as a pink-cheeked Melissa bounced into his office.

'Devdeep said you were looking for me,' she said. She'd already had a bit of a spat with Devdeep, and she was all set to do battle. 'I got little delayed because there wasn't a single cab on the roads today. There's some kind of a strike. I'd have called and told someone if I'd known you needed to talk to me.' She came to an abrupt halt, realising that it sounded as if she was making excuses. *Damn*, she'd wanted to come across as being completely cool and in charge of the situation.

Samir waited patiently till she was done. 'I asked where you were because I was looking around for familiar faces,' he said. 'I didn't see you all of last week.'

She was even prettier than he'd remembered—large, expressive chocolate-brown eyes in a piquant little face framed by masses of spun-silk hair. Right now, she looked defensive, and a lot less fiery than when he'd first met her, and he smiled at her reassuringly. The last thing he wanted was to terrorise the junior members of what he suspected was already a very apprehensive team.

Unfortunately Samir's reassuring smile had the effect of making Melissa's knees go just a little wobbly, and she took a few seconds to regroup before she said, 'I was in a creative writing workshop last week. Brian suggested it, actually—he felt that it'd help with my work.'

'That's OK,' Samir said, but Melissa still hesitated.

'I paid for it myself,' she volunteered.

At that, Samir looked up. 'I think it would have made more sense for the agency to pay if Brian asked you to take the workshop,' he said crisply. 'I'll speak to someone about it. And at some point I'd like you to take me through what you do—I'll drop you a line and schedule a time. Is there something else you'd like to talk about now?'

Melissa's slightly belligerent expression had vanished, but she still looked as if she wanted to get something off her chest.

'Um, he mightn't have told you, but it's Devdeep's birthday today,' she said. 'Brian's secretary normally orders a cake, but this time she wasn't sure what to do, so…'

'She can order a cake,' Samir said. 'You know what? It'd help if you could spread the word—for now everything continues as usual. I'll be making changes, but they'll take time, and they'll definitely not be about things like birthday cakes and what time people land up in office.'

Melissa's eyes narrowed, but she didn't say anything, whisking herself out of his office instead. In spite of his brusqueness there was a magnetic pull about Samir that was difficult to ignore. OK, *magnetic pull* was a really cheesy way of putting it, but that was how it felt. He was dressed casually, probably with the intention of blending in with the agency staff—but even in a linen shirt and faded jeans he exuded an aura of sheer masculine power that was difficult to ignore.

'He said you should order the cake, Kash,' she told Samir's secretary on her way back to her desk. 'Tell me when it's here and we'll set up the pantry for a party.'

Devdeep was dreadfully embarrassed by the fuss.

'He'll think we're completely flaky,' he protested, when Melissa and Kash told him.

'Nonsense, even the president celebrates her birthday,' Melissa said briskly. 'Samir won't think you're flaky at all, and if he does we'll put cockroaches in his room and spit in his water jug.'

'Thanks for warning me,' a dry voice said behind her, and Melissa jumped.

There he was, standing right behind her—all six foot two inches of scorching hot masculinity—and for the first time in her life Melissa found herself completely tongue-tied.

Devdeep turned a bright purple and said, 'She was just joking, sir, of course we'd do nothing of the sort.'

'Joking, was she?' Samir gave her a long look that didn't betray an iota of what he was thinking. 'Many happy returns of the day, Devdeep. And you can call me Samir. I haven't been knighted yet—and "sir" is a bit over the top, don't you think?'

Devdeep was still in the midst of a rather incoherent reply when Samir interrupted.

'Can I speak to you for a bit, Melissa?'

'If you were trying to put him at ease it didn't work,' Melissa muttered once they were out of earshot. 'Soon he'll be thanking you for allowing him to breathe the same air as you.'

At that Samir finally laughed. 'I can see I've been set up as a bit of an ogre, haven't I?'

Melissa looked him squarely in the eyes. 'No, you haven't,' she said. 'Brian decided to sell you the agency, and we trust his judgement. But you sitting in your room and poring over financial statements day after day isn't making people feel very confident.'

'Right,' Samir said. 'I guess I should have explained that I'm only handling the take-over—I'll have someone else actually managing the agency once I've got it fully integrated into Maximus. Look, Brian told me I could trust you to call things as they are. And that you'd be discreet even though you're one of the younger members of the team.'

Melissa nodded in what she hoped was a suitably responsible and discreet manner. So far in every interaction with Samir she'd come across as being a lot more immature and irresponsible than she actually was, and she was keen to correct the impression before he wrote her off as a complete airhead. Staying calm and focussed was difficult, though, with the completely unexpected effect that he was having on her.

'So it'd help if you told me exactly what people are worried about,' he said, leading the way into his room. 'I plan to address the team tomorrow, but I want to get my bearings first.'

'The older guys think you'll sack them,' she said bluntly. 'Especially the copywriters who work on regional languages. And people like me are worried that we'll no longer be doing the kind of work Brian trained us for—we'll just be churning out run-of-the-mill advertising. And a few, like Devdeep, just want to know how they can impress you and get promoted as soon as possible.'

Samir raised an eyebrow, and she went on.

'I'm not criticising him. He's probably the most sensible of the lot, and he has a wife and two kids to think of. It's just that for the rest of us there was a reason we joined Mendonca's, and the reason's now gone.'

'The work you're talking about,' Samir said. 'Could I see some of the things the agency's done in the past?'

'It's all around you!' Melissa exclaimed, but then the bare walls of the room registered. 'It's been taken down,' she said in surprise. 'Brian had all our best work framed and put up on the walls. And there were the awards and certificates we won...'

She sounded distinctly upset now, and Samir found himself explaining.

'I can't work in clutter,' he said. 'I didn't really look at the walls last time I was here, but I asked for the office to be cleared out completely before I joined. I assume Brian took the ads home.'

He was probably right—Brian had been inordinately proud of the collection of award-winning ads his walls had been plastered with and it was more than likely he hadn't wanted to leave them behind. It felt a little as if the soul of the agency had been torn away, Melissa thought, and then gave herself a quick mental shake. Brian was gone, and agonising over the past wasn't going to do her any good.

'There are soft copies of everything saved on the common drive that we all have access to,' she said briskly. 'I can show you if you like.'

She went around to his side of the table so that she could show him where the ads were stored.

As he turned the laptop, his hand touched hers briefly, and she pulled away as if from an electric shock. His lips tightened imperceptibly, making her flush. For a few seconds she'd forgotten that she was dealing with a rather dangerously good-looking man, and the sudden jolt of attraction had made her react stupidly.

'So, the ads are here,' she muttered, pointing at the screen. 'I'll…um…leave you to it, then.'

He looked up. 'Which one is the ad you wrote—the one Brian said was nominated for an award?'

'It's in the Robinson folder,' she said. 'The third one.'

He pulled the ad up onto the screen and looked at it silently for a while. It was a text-only ad for a range of baby products, and she'd written it from the point of view of a first-time mum. It was charming, and a little whimsical, and it wasn't really an ad in the traditional sense because it didn't talk about the products at all—it just said 'Happy Mother's Day' and the brand name at the end.

'Interesting,' Samir said. 'Any idea on how it impacted sales?'

Melissa stared at him as if he'd suddenly grown a second head. 'It doesn't work that way,' she protested. 'Ads like these make customers connect with the brand. There's no immediate effect on sales.'

'Right…' he said, but he was evidently not convinced. 'Always helps to have sales figures, though.'

It took all Melissa's willpower not to snap at him. 'I work on the creative side,' she said finally. 'It's the client servicing guys who work on the numbers.'

'You're not curious enough to ask for them?'

'I did ask!' she said. 'The sales figures were good, but I've forgotten exactly what percent they went up by. Devdeep would have the details.'

Samir didn't react, and she wondered if he'd even heard what she'd said. He was gazing intently at a spreadsheet now, his brows narrowed in concentration. In spite of her annoyance, one part of Melissa's brain noted that he managed to look very, very hot in an intense, brooding kind of way. Even when he clearly found his spreadsheet more fascinating than her ad.

She moved towards the door in what she hoped was an unobtrusive manner, and her hand was on the doorknob when he looked up, his rather stern features lightened by a genuine smile.

'It's a great ad, by the way,' he said. 'I can see why Brian thought so highly of you.'

The smile made his eyes crinkle up at the corners—suddenly he seemed a lot more human and approachable, like a movie star morphing into the local college football hero. Except that he was far more potently male than the average college heartthrob, and Melissa felt her breath come a little faster.

'Thank you,' she said, all her usual poise deserting her. 'I'll…um…I'll see you around, then, OK?'

She slipped out of the door, but it was a few minutes before Samir went back to his spreadsheet.

CHAPTER TWO

'WHERE IS EVERYONE?'

Melissa looked up. 'Devdeep and Shivani are in Goa for the ad awards,' she said. 'The rest of us are all here. As in they're around,' she added as Samir surveyed the empty cubicles and raised an eyebrow. 'They've gone for breakfast, I think.'

Samir had been travelling, and it was a week since she'd last seen him. He looked tanned and fit and almost good enough to eat.

His brow creased in a frown. 'If you wrote the ad why aren't *you* on your way to Goa? Didn't Devdeep think of taking you along?'

'He did.' Melissa bit her lip. She didn't like Devdeep much, but the poor man wasn't to blame for this particular situation.

'And you decided not to go?' Samir sounded positively incredulous now.

There was no way out of this other than admitting the embarrassing truth. 'I…um…I have a slight phobia about flying,' Melissa said in a rush. 'The trains were booked solid because it's a long weekend, and Devdeep said that going alone on a bus might not be safe.'

'And a bullock cart would take too much time, I assume?' Samir said, his lips twitching. 'How about cycling to Goa? Did you consider that?'

'Very funny,' Melissa said crossly. 'I did want to go. I'm just trying to tell you that it didn't work out.'

Too late, she realised that snapping at the new agency head was probably not very bright of her. Luckily, he looked more amused than offended.

'You could come with me,' Samir said, taking even himself by surprise. 'I'm driving down—I'm leaving early tomorrow morning and I can pick you up. Where d'you live?'

'Colaba,' Melissa said, trying not to gape at him. 'But are you sure?'

'Yes, I am,' Samir said, though he was wondering whether he'd suddenly gone quite mad.

There was no way Melissa could know it, but he never volunteered to spend time with a woman—let alone thirteen hours closeted with one in a car. For a second he wondered whether he should retract the offer, but there was no way he could back out of it without coming across as being incredibly rude.

Oh, really, Razdan? he said wryly to himself as he took down her address and mobile number. As if the fear of being thought rude had ever stopped him in the past.

Melissa was ready on the dot of six, perched on her bed. It had taken some time to decide what to wear—too dressed up and he might think she was making a play for him—too casual and he mightn't want to be seen with her. She'd finally settled for denim cut-offs with a long-sleeved white cotton shirt and sat down to wait.

Her phone rang at a quarter past six, and she picked it up, her heart suddenly beating a lot faster.

'Hi,' she said tentatively.

'Ready to leave?' he asked, not bothering to return her greeting. 'I'm in a black car, right outside your hostel gate.'

And what a car it was. Melissa found it difficult to take her eyes off the sleek, powerfully built machine. Then she saw Samir, and her mouth went dry with longing. So far she'd only seen him in office clothes—in an open-necked T-shirt and cargo shorts he looked even hotter than he did in formals.

She took a deep breath before she crossed the road to join him. Letting him know how much he affected her was a bad, *bad* idea.

'Thanks for doing this,' she said politely as she got into the car. 'I'm really looking forward to the awards festival, even if we don't win anything.'

'You're welcome,' Samir said.

She looked very young and appealing, with a little rucksack slung over one shoulder, and her hair held back with an Alice band, but there was something innocently sensual in the way she

twisted her slim body around to toss the rucksack into the backseat. Her hair fell over her
shoulder, and he caught a whiff of a fresh floral
scent that made him want to reach out and
touch—it took a strong effort of will to remain
unaffected by her nearness.

'Car rules,' he said, passing her a bottle of
water and hoping she hadn't noticed him looking at her. 'Seat belt on at all times. No eating
in the car. And absolutely no attempts to change
the music.'

Melissa peeked at his face to see if he was
joking. Apparently not. With uncharacteristic
meekness she tugged at the seat belt—the seat
belt, however, seemed to have firm ideas of its
own, and refused to budge.

'I can't—' she started to say, and with an impatient shrug he leaned across to help her.

Melissa immediately froze. Her first thought
was that he was much...much *larger* than she'd
thought he was—the second was that if she
moved just an inch she'd be touching him, and
there was something terribly tempting about

the thought. Then there was the smell of his aftershave… Woody, with a slight hint of citrus, it teased at her nostrils as he released the seat belt from where it was snagged behind her seat.

'Here—it's free now,' he said.

He moved away from her, apparently completely unaffected by her proximity. Oh, well, maybe her three-hundred-rupee perfume and demure clothes just didn't do it for him. Despite herself, she felt a little miffed. Sure, he was a hotshot executive and all that, but she would have liked him to take just a *little* interest in her as a woman. And her own reaction to him was annoying—she wasn't usually the swooning-over-a-hot-man type. Then common sense reasserted itself. Samir was undeniably gorgeous, and there was absolutely nothing to be ashamed of in finding him lust-worthy. As long as she restricted herself to a purely aesthetic appreciation of his hotness she'd be fine.

Samir put the car into gear, his lips thinning. The tiny gasp that Melissa had let out when he'd leaned over her hadn't escaped him, and he was regretting his offer of a lift more than ever.

Melissa was wrong about his reactions—one look at her long, tanned brown legs and her slim but curvy figure and everything male in him had responded enthusiastically. Being older and more experienced, he was just a great deal better at concealing his reactions.

They were both silent as the car sped through nearly empty streets all the way past Dadar and Chembur, and over the creek at Vashi. The sky was beginning to lighten, and the city looked as if it had just been through an extensive makeover. It was a wonder the amount of difference the lack of traffic and pollutants made.

They were nearly at the Pune expressway when Melissa finally spoke.

'Can we stop for a bit?' she asked.

Samir gave her an impatient look. 'I'd like to get on the expressway before traffic builds up,' he said. 'Can you hold on till we get to the first toll? There's a food plaza there, and it's only around an hour off.'

'I'm hungry,' she said in a small voice.

She'd missed dinner the night before, and the hostel breakfast service only started at seven in the morning. It was all very well for Samir, she thought resentfully. He probably had a retinue of cooks who would have a piping hot breakfast on the table even if he decided to leave home at four a.m.

Unwilling to explain that she was actually feeling light-headed with hunger, she said, 'And I need to use the loo. Right now.' *Ha*—that wasn't something he could argue with.

It didn't look as if he was fooled, but he pulled into a burger joint.

'D'you want anything?' she asked, and he shook his head.

'I'll wait outside,' he said.

'I'll be quick,' she promised, and darted into the restaurant.

The queues were long, and after almost an hour in the car Melissa found that she was feeling distinctly dizzy—her ears were buzzing, and by the time she got to the head of the queue she knew she was in no state to order.

'You can go ahead,' she muttered to the woman behind her.

'Oh, thanks,' the woman said gratefully—she had several kids in tow, and they had been bouncing with eagerness to order their second round of burgers. Then she looked a little more closely at Melissa. 'Are you feeling all right?' she asked.

Melissa had just enough time to shake her head before black spots started dancing in front of her eyes.

Samir finished sending out a couple of urgent e-mails on his smart phone and looked up, thinking that as they'd stopped anyway a coffee might be a good idea.

The restaurant had plate-glass windows on three sides, and just as he was about to start towards it he saw Melissa sink gracefully into the arms of the middle-aged woman standing next to her. He took the next few steps at a run, bursting into the restaurant just as the woman helped Melissa to a sofa.

'What's happened to her?' he asked, his voice harsh, and the woman looked up in undisguised relief.

'Oh, are you with her? Thank heavens. I didn't know what to do! I think she's just feeling a little faint. Rishu, give me that soda! And the rest of you kids, go and sit with Vishal Uncle. I'll be with you in a minute.'

The kid she'd addressed gave up the drink without a peep, though he looked rather upset. Melissa was trying to sit up now, and the woman held the paper cup to her lips.

'Thanks,' Melissa said after a few sips. 'Sorry about this.'

'No worries,' the woman said comfortably, straightening up. 'I'll be right over there in case you need help,' she told Samir. 'I think she's OK now, but a check-up might be in order once you guys get home.'

Melissa thanked her again, and gave Samir an awkward look once the woman went away.

'I'm so sorry,' she said. 'This hasn't ever happened before.'

He was frowning. 'Do you feel OK otherwise? Should I take you back to Mumbai? That
woman was right—you need to see a doctor.'

But Melissa was already shaking her head.
'There's no need,' she said. 'I think I'll be fine
once I eat something.'

His frown deepened. 'Did you have breakfast?' he asked abruptly, and she shook her
head. 'Dinner last night?'

Feeling hideously embarrassed, she shook her
head again.

'Why not? What time did you leave work?'

'Nine-forty,' she muttered. 'The hostel curfew
is at ten on week-nights, so I had to rush back.
And I forgot that I was out of instant noodles.'

'We'll talk after I get some food into you,'
Samir said grimly. The interested onlookers in
the restaurant waved him to the head of the
queue and he came back with a chicken burger
and a milkshake.

Melissa took the burger, but shook her head

at the milkshake. 'Lactose intolerant,' she explained before biting into the juicy bun. The rush of flavours had her feeling a little sick for a few seconds, but the nausea soon receded and she tore enthusiastically into the burger.

'I'll get you another one,' Samir muttered, rejoining the queue. It took him a little longer this time, but he came back with another burger, a soft drink and a coffee for himself.

'So did you have lunch yesterday?' he asked conversationally.

Melissa paused mid-bite. 'I did,' she said cautiously. 'At least I think I did. Yes, of course! I remember. Dubeyji ordered a plate of *pavbhaji*, and I shared it with him.'

'You *do* know that you're allowed time off for meals, don't you?' he asked. 'And that the agency won't shut down if you leave early enough to have dinner?'

She laughed. 'Yes, of course,' she said. 'This must be the first time I've missed dinner because of work. It's just that I hadn't originally planned on going to Goa, and I had a bunch of stuff to finish before I could go.'

'So essentially it's my fault?' Samir said.

Melissa said, 'Oh, no!' before she realised he was teasing her. Blushing hotly, she buried her face in her paper cup of soda.

'That's better,' he said. 'Finally, you have some colour in your cheeks.'

'I can't have colour in my cheeks. I'm too brown,' she retorted.

'Rubbish,' he said, and lightly patted her arm, sending a little tingle through her, all the way down to her toes. 'Tell me when you're feeling better and we'll leave. No hurry.'

'I'm good to go,' she announced, bouncing to her feet.

Samir put a steadying arm around her. 'Careful, don't jump around,' he said. 'We can't have you collapsing again.'

'I won't,' she protested, intensely conscious of the strong arm around her waist.

He didn't let her go till he'd handed her into the passenger seat of the car. Even then he waited till she was properly belted in before he went around to the driver's seat and got in.

'I need you to let me know if you're feeling the slightest bit unwell,' he said. 'And I'm relaxing the no food in the car rule—you can have what you want as long as you don't collapse again.'

In spite of her cynicism about rich playboys Melissa felt rather touched by Samir's awkwardly expressed concern. It had been a while since someone had cared enough about her to fuss. Even if the fussing was being done in an off-hand, ultra-macho kind of way.

Samir connected his MP3 player to the car's music system before they drove off. Melissa had assumed he'd be into rock or heavy metal, but surprisingly most of the tracks were *ghazals* or Bollywood oldies.

She hummed along to some of her favourite songs—she had a sweet and unexpectedly strong voice, and Samir found himself listening more to her than to the original song playing through the car speakers. She seemed so completely unselfconscious that he felt himself relaxing a little. It was a surprisingly liberating change, being with someone who didn't have an agenda either to impress him or to get information out of him.

'Who do you keep texting?' he asked as he watched her type out her third or fourth message since she'd stepped into the car. 'You're like a stenographer on steroids, the way you keep hammering into that phone.'

The second the words were out of his mouth he realised that he'd let himself relax a bit too much. Making personal remarks to someone he hardly knew was completely uncharacteristic of him—no wonder she was staring at him as if he'd grown a third eye in the middle of his forehead like Lord Shiva.

'I'm sorry,' he said immediately. 'None of my business—forget I asked.'

Melissa laughed, showing a perfect set of teeth, small, white and very even.

'I'm texting a friend back at the hostel,' she said. 'We just passed the turn-off for that new amusement park that's been built here. One of the girls is coming next weekend with her latest boyfriend—she wanted to know how long it would take to get here.'

'Won't it be more suitable for kids?'

'No, there are rides for adults as well. And the tickets are quite expensive—it's a rather cool place for a first date. For regular people, I mean.'

He raised his eyebrows. 'As opposed to *irregular* people like me?'

Refusing to be embarrassed, Melissa said, 'You know what I mean. If you took a girl out for a date you'd probably go to the theatre, or to a restaurant in a five-star hotel. The guys my friends date don't even own cars—they don't have many places to take a girl to.'

'Where does *your* boyfriend take you?' Samir asked, half jokingly and half because he wanted to know for sure that she was unattached. This asking questions thing was pretty addictive—especially when the other person was as cool about it as Melissa.

'I don't have a boyfriend,' she said, but there was something rather weird in the way she said it, as if she was mocking herself.

Samir wouldn't normally have given himself credit for being perceptive, but instinctively he knew he needed to change the topic.

'Do you like your job?' he asked, and she gave him a startled look.

'Yes,' she said cautiously, and then, 'Why? Is there any chance I mightn't have it any longer?'

This time Samir looked startled. 'Not that I know of. I'm not making any changes in the agency structure—not for now at least. And when I do it definitely won't be at your level.'

'Too junior?' she asked, giving him a cheeky wink. 'Or is my salary not big enough to dent the profit figures?'

It probably wasn't, but Samir could hardly say so without sounding impossibly condescending. He hesitated for a second, and she let him off the hook by jumping to another subject.

'I just found a pack of candy in my purse,'

she announced. 'I'd forgotten I had them. You want one?'

Samir shook his head.

'They're nice,' she persisted. 'Tamarind and sugar.'

He took his eyes off the road for a second and glanced at the small packet in her hand. 'I haven't seen that stuff in years,' he said. 'They used to hand them out on flights when I was in college—I used to stuff my pockets full of them.'

'Does that mean you want one, then?'

'Yes, please. But you'll have to unwrap it first. I can't take my hands off the wheel.'

She took a sweet out of its wrapper and waited for him to take it from her. They were near Lonavla now, and at a rather tricky section of the road. There was no way Samir could let go of the wheel, and the candy had begun to melt in Melissa's palm.

'This is going all sticky,' she warned, and then, feeling very daring, 'Should I pop it in your mouth?'

He nodded, and she immediately wished she hadn't been quite so forward. He parted his perfectly sculpted lips a little and she leaned across to pop the sweet into his mouth. The candy stuck to her fingers for a few seconds and finally he sucked it off, the feel of his lips and tongue incredibly erotic against her skin.

Pulse racing, Melissa sat back and shot him a covert look. He was as unruffled as ever, but there was a slight smile playing about his lips. Until that instant she hadn't thought of him as someone she could actually get involved with. There were so many reasons, but right now she couldn't think clearly about them. All she could think about was how easy it would be to lean a little closer to him, breathe in the heady scent of his cologne, drop a kiss on his lips when he next turned to speak to her…

And probably make him drive the car into a road divider and kill them both. She sighed. Having a pragmatic side was all very well, but it did have a bad habit of popping up and ruining her best fantasies. So, all right, perhaps trying to seduce him while he was driving wasn't a good plan.

She stole another look at Samir. He had the kind of good looks that grew on you. The first time she'd seen him she'd thought he looked gorgeous, but rather cold—not her type at all. But the more time she spent with him, the more she noticed things—like the way his smile reached all the way up to his eyes when he was amused, and how he pushed his unruly hair off his forehead in an unconsciously sexy gesture every few minutes.

At around the end of the expressway Samir pulled out an electronic tablet and handed it to Melissa. 'I've plotted the route on this—the car's GPS isn't terribly reliable in this part of the world. Will you keep an eye on it to make sure we're on track?'

Melissa looked at him in horror. 'Don't you know where you're going?' she asked.

He laughed. 'Goa,' he said. 'We'll get there

eventually. Sooner rather than later if you're a good navigator.'

She proved to be an excellent navigator—though more than once Samir found himself getting distracted by the way her hair fell across her face as she pored over the map, and the way her brow wrinkled up with concentration.

Even the first time he'd met her he'd thought that she had lovely eyes, but it was only now that he noticed the flawlessness of her dusky complexion and the near perfect shape of her lips. Her slim figure curved enticingly at all the right places, and in the few seconds he'd held her after she fainted he hadn't been able to help thinking how soft her skin was, and how right she felt in his arms.

'We'll be in Kolhapur in another hour or so,' Melissa said, effectively breaking into his thoughts. 'Are we stopping there or going straight on?'

'We could stop for lunch,' Samir said. 'There's another burger place on the highway, and a couple of coffee shops as well.'

Melissa wrinkled up her nose. 'I had two burgers for breakfast,' she said. 'I don't think I can look one in the face for a while. Can we go somewhere else? I've often seen Vegetable Kolhapur on restaurant menus—would it be a kind of speciality here?'

'Along with Kolhapuri *chappals*,' Samir agreed solemnly.

Melissa made a face at him. 'I wasn't planning to buy footwear. But do let's stop somewhere in the city.'

It would add another hour to the drive at least, but Samir complied. After Melissa's fainting fit his attitude towards her had changed. Not normally indulgent towards other people's whims, he found himself unaccountably wanting to fall in with whatever she wanted.

They chose a small restaurant in the centre of the city—the food was spicy, and not really to his taste, but it was worth the delay just to see Melissa savour the meal. Unlike the perpetually dieting women Samir normally dated, she genuinely enjoyed her food, just about stopping short of licking her fingers after polishing off everything on her plate.

'Dessert?' he asked after she was done. 'There's ice creams and *gulab jamun*. Or, no, you can't have the ice cream if you're lactose-intolerant. *Gulab jamun*?'

It was the first time anyone had actually re-membered she was lactose intolerant—people who'd known her for years, including her own sister-in-law, continued to ply her with milk-shakes and ice cream every time they met. Maybe he just had a good memory, but she couldn't help feeling a little flattered.

'*Gulab jamun*,' she said.

Samir watched her as she dug a spoon into a *gulab jamun*, golden syrup gushing out of the round sweet. It was a messy dish to eat, and she paused a couple of times to lick the syrup off her lips. His eyes were automatically drawn to her lush mouth and the way her little pink tongue ran over its contours. She was the first woman he'd met whose simplest gesture ended up being unconsciously sexy. Or, then again, maybe he was just turning into a horny old man.

'How old are you?' he asked abruptly.

'Twenty-four,' Melissa said, and her brow furrowed up as she polished off the last bit of *gulab jamun*. 'Why?'

Why, indeed? She looked so young that for a second he'd wondered if she was underage.

'I was thinking about the ad you wrote,' he said. 'I'd assumed it was written by an older woman—someone with kids.'

'Oh, that,' she said, looking embarrassed. 'I spent a lot of time with my sister-in-law after my nephew was born. She didn't have anyone else to help her with the baby.'

'Still, it was a very insightful piece of work. I'll be surprised if it doesn't win something.'

Feeling more and more embarrassed, Melissa said, 'Has Brian been brainwashing you?'

Samir laughed, his eyes crinkling up at the corners in a particularly attractive way. 'He happened to mention it a few times. But I don't get easily influenced by other people's opinions.

Are you done? We should leave if we want to get to Goa before it's dark.'

He put a hand under her elbow to guide her out of the restaurant and Melissa felt all her fantasies come rushing back in full force. Of course he was probably just being polite. Or he was worried she'd keel over and faint once again, and he'd have to carry her out on his shoulder. Either way, her insides were doing weird things at his touch, and the temptation to touch him in return was immense.

She tried to kill the fantasy by imagining his reaction. Shock? Embarrassment? Then she remembered the feel of his lips on her fingers as he'd taken the sticky candy from them, and she couldn't help thinking that maybe, just maybe, he'd reciprocate. Bend down and kiss her. Tangle his big strong hands in her hair and tip her head back to get better access to her lips…

'Melissa?'

Brought back to earth with a thump, she realised he was holding the car door open for her.

'Sorry,' she said, sliding into her seat quickly.

'You're a complete daydreamer, aren't you?' he asked, looking rather amused as he got into the driver's seat. 'What were you thinking about?'

Ha—wouldn't you like to know? Melissa felt like saying. Maybe some day she'd actually be confident enough to come back with the truth when a man like Samir asked her a question like that. Unfortunately, as of now, she was less than halfway there.

'Just stuff,' she said after a pause.

'Random stuff?'

'Oh, very random.' He'd sounded a bit sceptical, and she felt she needed to justify herself. 'As random as Brownian motion—you know, that thing they show you in school…dust motes being tossed around by invisible molecules… my mind's a bit like that.'

He gave her a long look, and she shook her head, laughing.

'Sorry, sorry. Rambling a bit there.'

'Just a bit,' he said, but his lips quirked up at the corners as if he was trying hard not to smile.

Melissa had a nasty feeling that he knew exactly what she'd been thinking about. She concentrated on her phone for a bit, replying to the various texts that had come in while they were at lunch. When she looked up they were on the highway again, going down a rather lovely stretch of road with sugarcane fields on both sides and rolling green hills on the horizon.

'Look at the bougainvillaea down the centre of the road—aren't they beautiful?'

Samir hadn't noticed the bougainvillaea other than as an unnecessary distraction—at her words, though, he gave them a quick glance.

'They're OK, I guess,' he said. 'Though they seem to be planted in any old order. White for a few hundred metres and then miles of pink, with a couple of yellows thrown in.'

'I thought that was the nicest thing about them,' she returned. 'They look as if they've just sprung up, not as if someone planned—' She stopped short as she took in Samir's less than interested expression. 'Sorry,' she said.

'The driving must be stressful, and here I am babbling about bougainvillaea.'

'And now you're making me feel guilty about being a grumpy old git,' Samir said wryly. 'I'm sorry—I'm not very good at noticing things.'

'I'm the opposite,' Melissa said, mock-mournfully. 'I notice everything. My head's chock-full of all kinds of unnecessary junk.'

'It'll all come in handy some day,' Samir said. 'You'll be brilliant if you're on a quiz show, one day, and they show you a picture of a road and ask you to identify it.'

The good stretch seemed to be over now, because the next turnoff they took was onto a road that barely deserved the name. It was pretty much a long stretch of potholes connected by little strips of tar, and Melissa winced as the car bounced up and down.

'Sorry,' Samir said, putting a brief steadying hand on her knee as they went over a particularly bad crater.

Even through the frayed denim of her cutoffs Melissa could feel the warm strength of his hand, and she began to feel a lot more positive about the state of the road. *Every cloud... et cetera, et cetera*, she thought, an involuntary grin coming to her lips.

Beginning to enjoy herself thoroughly now, she let the next crater bounce her sideways so that she landed on his shoulder. 'Oops,' she said. 'You need to drive more carefully, Samir.'

Samir gave her a sideways look but didn't say anything. That last bounce had been deliberate, he was sure of it, but she seemed to be doing it for fun. He was used to women saying and doing things to win his approval—Melissa was something else altogether. She was definitely as attracted to him as he was to her, but she was treating the whole situation as a bit of a joke.

'I'm rolling the windows down,' she announced when they came to a stretch where, wonder of wonders, there was an actual repair crew busily laying a new layer of tar on top of the existing apology for a road. 'I love the smell of fresh tar.'

She didn't wait for his permission, and Samir

wondered what she'd have said if he told her he was allergic to dust and tarry smells. He wasn't, but if he had been she'd probably have found that funny as well, he thought resignedly.

'Did you notice how the colour of the soil changes between states?' she was asking. 'It was brown while we were in Maharashtra, then it turned black near the Karnataka border—and in Goa it's brick-red.'

Samir shook his head. 'I wouldn't notice something like that even if there were mile-high signs telling me about it.'

Melissa didn't say anything, but it was clear she thought that not noticing anything sounded incredibly boring.

He gave her a quick smile. 'Though I *do* notice that you have a dirt smear on your cheek,' he said, stroking the offending item lightly with the back of his hand. 'That comes from having your nose stuck out of the window.'

'*Touché,*' Melissa said and grinned as she rubbed the smudge off. 'I've always wanted to say that to someone, only I've never met anyone swanky enough to speak French to.'

'I might be swanky, but I can at least speak Hindi,' Samir remarked. 'You're jabbering away in English all the time.'

'In the agency? That's because poor old Dubeyji almost had a heart attack when I tried speaking to him in Hindi. Apparently my grammar's all wrong, and I sound terribly rude.'

'You sound terribly rude even when you're speaking English,' Samir murmured.

She punched him lightly in the arm. 'Ouch, way too musclebound,' she said, pretending to nurse the knuckles on her right hand. 'You should go easy on the gym—live life a little. You'd make a much nicer punching bag if you were flabby.'

'What a nice thought,' he said, laughing. 'But I think I'll stick to my gym routine. And you might want to concentrate on that map—there's a town coming up and I've no idea whether to go through it or around it.'

'You have reached your destination,' the smug voice-over on the map informed them a few hours later.

'Except that we're in the middle of freaking nowhere,' Samir muttered.

After telling them to take a right turn towards the Uttorda beach the map had carefully led them to a cul-de-sac, with the beach on one side and a grove of coconut trees on the other.

A man passed by them, whistling cheerfully, and Melissa rolled down the window. 'Is there a hotel nearby?' she asked him in Konkani.

'Lots,' the man said. 'This is Goa—not the Thar desert. Any particular one that you might be looking for?'

Melissa consulted the name on the map and told him.

'You'll need to go back the way you came for a kilometre or so,' he said. 'Turn right at the big purple house and you'll see the signs for the hotel.'

'Well, at least it got us this far,' Samir said in resigned tones as he switched off the tablet a few minutes later. 'Though I wish our friend back there had given clearer directions—every third house here is purple. It didn't occur to me earlier—you're Goan, aren't you? Don't you have family here?'

'They all live very far away,' Melissa said. 'Um, should I call Devdeep or someone who's already arrived and get proper directions?'

'You'd need to explain where we are first,' Samir said. 'Let's do the old-fashioned thing and ask a real live human being.'

The next 'real live human being' they met fortunately knew the area well, and within ten minutes they were pulling into the hotel grounds.

'Thanks once again,' Melissa said once they'd arrived. She was feeling unaccountably shy, and automatically reverted to formality. 'You didn't have to give me a lift, but you did, and I had a great time.'

For a few seconds Samir looked down at her, his dark eyes mesmerising in their intensity. Then a hostess bustled up to them with a tray of welcome drinks and the moment passed.

'I'll see you around, then,' Samir said, taking his room keys from the bellboy and slinging his bag over his shoulder. 'Some of the other guys are already here—you could call them and catch up maybe.'

Was that a subtle way of telling her not to expect to hang around with *him*? Melissa felt absurdly upset at the thought as she watched him stride away.

Just as he was about to step out of the lobby, he turned around. 'Melissa?'

'Yes?' she said.

'Make sure you eat your meals on time, OK?' he said, smiling a crooked little smile. 'No fainting when you're called up to receive the award.'

'OK,' she said.

It was only when she reached her room and looked into the mirror that she realised that she was still smiling goofily.

'Idiot woman,' she told her reflection crossly. 'It was fun, but the trip's over now. You'll be lucky if he pays any attention to you at all after this.'

Her reflection looked back at her just as crossly, and she gave it a wry grin.

'I know. I liked him too. But he's my boss—

I can't chase after him. Time for a cold shower now, OK?'

She moved away from the mirror, her good humour at least partly restored. She'd decided a couple of years back not to take men too seriously, and so far she'd managed to stick by it.

Wandering into the bathroom, she hummed softly under her breath as she turned on the taps. *Eek*, the cold water was really, *really* cold. Maybe a lukewarm shower would do just as well without giving her pneumonia.

By the time she was done with ironing an impossibly crushed pair of shorts, tucking her hair under a shower cap and actually going ahead and taking a shower, it was past six. It took her a few seconds to give her hair a brushing and pull on a yellow spaghetti strap top over the neatly ironed shorts. Once she was done, she gave herself a quick look in the mirror and headed off to the beach.

There was an enthusiastic game of cricket in progress between Devdeep and a couple of other guys from Mendonca's and a bunch of youngsters from another agency. Pretty much the entire Mumbai advertising fraternity seemed to be in Goa, either infesting the beach or helping the state economy along by drinking larger quantities of beer and *feni*.

'Join us!' one of the younger cricket players in the group yelled out to Melissa.

'You're supposed to play volleyball on the beach, not cricket,' she yelled back. 'Losers!'

'Leave her alone—girls can't play cricket,' one of the surlier members of the team grunted.

'Oh, can't they?' Melissa said, promptly kicking off her sandals and joining them.

The sand felt good under her feet—it had been a long while since she'd gone barefoot. Mumbai had its fair share of beaches, but they were crowded and often dirty.

'You can field,' the surly man said. 'Just don't get in the way of the other fielders.'

Melissa didn't say anything—just waited till the luckless batsman hit a ball in her direction. She moved across the sand like a guided missile, leaving Mr Surly and the others gaping as she caught the ball in mid-air and whirled around to knock down a wicket. Clearly unused to running in the sand, the batsmen were only halfway down the crease—they didn't stand a chance.

'Out,' she said with satisfaction. 'I think I'll bowl next, thank you.'

There was a second of stunned silence, and then 'her' team started cheering madly. The bowler was the man who'd first called out to her, and he relinquished his place to her gladly. He was a nice-looking chap, with curly hair and an impish grin, and Melissa liked him immediately.

'Down here for the ad fest?' he asked as he handed over the ball.

Melissa nodded.

'I'm Akash,' he said. 'Would you like to catch up later? Figure out which of our entries is likely to get a gold in the festival?'

'Akash, stop hitting on the bowler,' one of the other players said.

'Yeah, Akash, there's no way she'd want to be seen with a loser like *you*,' another chimed in.

Melissa gave the guy a saucy grin. 'I'll tell you once the game is over,' she said.

She wasn't in the least attracted to him, but it made sense hanging out with a bunch of people her own age rather than hanging around and hoping Samir would come and find her.

CHAPTER THREE

AFTER THIRTEEN HOURS behind the wheel, every muscle in Samir's body felt stiff—he was supposed to be at a 'networking' session, but it sounded so incredibly boring that he'd made a flimsy excuse and escaped to his room.

Once there, he changed into running shorts and a dry fit T-shirt before slipping on his running shoes. A run would make up for the gym session he'd missed in the morning. Hopefully it would also get him tired enough to stop thinking about Melissa's lissom body.

Used to running on Tarmac, or on the jogging track at the Mumbai race course, Samir avoided the beach. The lane outside the hotel had a fair bit of traffic, and he turned off into a by-lane as soon as he could. There was much less traffic here, other than the occasional cow or motorcycle, and he was able to build up a decent pace.

Running always helped clear his head, and he was able to think a little more rationally about his reaction to Melissa. She was an attractive woman, but he'd been seeing her around the office for weeks now and had never turned to give her a second look. Maybe it had been the effect of being thrown together with her for several hours—yes, that had to be it, he decided. And her fainting fit in the morning had aroused his protective instincts.

The sun was on the verge of setting when Samir glanced at his watch. He had been running for forty-five minutes—a little short of his normal hour, but perfectly respectable. He was opposite one of the public entrances to the Uttorda beach, and he slowed to a walk.

He felt strangely reluctant to go back to the hotel. It had been only a couple of years since he'd started actually running the companies his family owned, and he wasn't yet used to the automatically deferential way the teams treated him. It was especially noticeable in Mendonca Advertising, because as a rule advertising peo-

ple were a lot less respectful of hierarchy—
Brian had been treated more like a well-loved
uncle than a boss.

Maybe the rumours that he was planning to
downsize accounted for it. People like Devdeep
were desperately trying to prove that they were
creative and revenue-focussed at the same time,
like a modern-day David Ogilvy and Jack Welch
rolled into one. And others, like Dubeyji, the
elderly man who managed their Hindi advertising, were openly resentful. If you wanted to
run a company successfully you couldn't keep
everyone happy—Brian had tried, and in the
process almost run the agency into the ground.

Green coconut water would be good, if he
could find someone selling it, he thought as he
made his way to the beach. There was a small
stall right at the entry to the beach, and he paid
for a coconut, sipping the delicate water through
a straw as he walked towards the sea. There was
a game of cricket in progress—and while the
teams seemed to have very little regard for the

rules of the game, they were evidently having the time of their lives.

Something vaguely familiar about one of the women playing caught his eye, and he automatically slowed down. She was slim, brown-skinned, with endless legs and flyaway hair, and he felt a jolt of recognition hit him as she turned to laugh at something one of the other players was saying.

In the next second Melissa caught sight of Samir, and she tossed the bat to the next player and came towards him.

'I just got run out,' she said, making a face. 'I'm brilliant at bowling and fielding—batting's not so good. though. Where were you? Jogging?'

'Running,' he said.

She probably didn't care if he'd been running or sprinting or playing hopscotch, but it seemed important to make the distinction. Jogging sounded like the kind of thing you did when you were forty and over the hill. Of course, to someone Melissa's age thirty might seem just as ancient.

She was looking at his shoes now, inspecting them as carefully as if she meant to buy them from him. 'You have proper running shoes,' she stated, sounding surprised. 'Everyone I know uses everything interchangeably—tennis shoes and football studs and running shoes.'

'Or they just run around barefoot,' Samir said, before he could help it.

Even covered in sand, her feet were very pretty, the nails painted a bright turquoise and a little silver anklet around one ankle. He'd been trying to keep his eyes off her legs and her small, pert breasts jiggling around under her yellow top, but her bare feet were pretty sexy as well.

Melissa made a face. Her spontaneous reaction when she'd seen Samir had been to come across to him—she'd forgotten what a sight she must look, with her muddy denim shorts, windswept hair and bare feet.

'I didn't bring proper shoes,' she said. 'And it

was a spur-of-the-moment thing, joining these guys—I was planning to go and splash around in the sea, so I wore beach slippers.'

'You can still do that,' Samir said. Out of the corner of his eye he spotted Devdeep, abandoning his wicketkeeper role to come towards them, and he wanted to escape. 'Come on—race you to the water.'

He won, of course, but she came a close second, retaliating by running into the water and splashing him while he stopped by the edge to take off his shoes and socks.

'Just you wait,' he said, grabbing her around the waist and swinging her bodily into the next wave.

Their actual physical contact was brief—his hands touched her waist for a few seconds, and then she was back on her feet, spluttering and laughing. For a few more seconds their eyes met—then a massive wave came rolling in, almost knocking Melissa off her feet, and the moment was lost.

When the water receded Melissa discovered

that her pavement store spaghetti strap top had taken the opportunity to turn completely transparent. Given that it was pale yellow, and that she'd chosen to wear a neon pink bra under it, the whole effect was a little B-grade Bollywood.

Samir was keeping his eyes studiously averted from her chest—great, that showed he was a gentleman—perversely, though, Melissa wanted to know if she had any effect on him at all. The flicker of interest she'd seen on the drive in had been so slight that she might have completely imagined it.

'Oops,' she said, looking down at herself. 'Need some help, here. I can't go back to the beach looking like India's answer to *Baywatch*. And no one handy to be rescued either.'

At that, Samir laughed. It wasn't a boastful comparison—in spite of her slim frame Melissa's bust offered fair competition to the world's most admired bathing beauties. He was having a hard time pretending to be indifferent.

'I can pretend to drown, if you'd like,' he offered. 'In the excitement you could slip away unnoticed.'

'It'd be more useful if you gave me your T-shirt,' she said, eyeing the beach apprehensively. The cricket game had wound up and the boys were heading purposefully towards the water.

Samir looked around and assessed the situation in a glance.

'Here you go,' he said, yanking the shirt over his head in a single fluid movement and tossing it to her. 'I've been running in it for an hour, though, and it's a mess. Not to mention the salt water.'

Melissa grabbed the shirt instinctively, but for a few seconds couldn't help gawking at him. His body more than lived up to expectations— in running shorts and nothing else he was all muscular chest and six-pack abs, and he looked like her favourite Bollywood star, only more real. When he frowned at her, she hastily pulled the shirt on.

Far from being 'a mess', the shirt smelt of

clean male sweat and salt water, and the sudden intimacy made her hormones go into overdrive. She had to look away for a few seconds to get her unruly pulse under control. The shirt was big on her, flapping damply around her thighs, but at least she no longer looked like Silk Smitha.

The boys were nearer the water now, and even though she was decently covered Melissa couldn't help wondering how she'd explain Samir's suddenly shirtless self and her own in-the-sea costume change.

'Maybe we should take a walk down the seashore,' Samir suggested, 'and head back to the hotel after the sun sets?'

'I think that's a good idea,' Melissa said, hoping her dusky skin concealed the rush of colour to her cheeks.

'Have you spoken to your relatives yet?' he asked as they walked a little farther down the beach.

He was feeling intensely aware of her nearness and the unconsciously sexy picture she made in her tiny denim shorts with her damp hair tumbling over her shoulders. He could understand the Portuguese sailors who'd landed on the Goa coast centuries ago and then stayed, beguiled by the beauty of the Goan women they'd met there. It was a fanciful thought, but maybe one of Melissa's ancestors had been among those women.

'I didn't carry my phone onto the beach,' Melissa said, and it took him a few seconds to connect her reply with the rather banal question he'd asked a few seconds earlier.

'You could go and meet them if you want,' he said. 'I have a car booked, but I'm not likely to use it. There's some stuff that's come up at Maximus that I need to sort out.'

'Thanks,' she said. 'I'll let you know if I manage to get in touch with them.'

She had no intention of doing anything of the sort, but there was no point getting into a lengthy and possibly boring explanation of how things actually stood between her and her family.

'Looks like someone's decided to get married on the beach,' Samir said a few minutes later, touching her lightly on the arm.

Melissa turned to look. It was a rather impressive tableau against the setting sun—the bride in a perfectly stunning off-the-shoulder wedding gown, with a train that dragged along the sand, and the more casually dressed groom in a white linen shirt and pale dress jeans. The only other people with them were a bridesmaid, a priest and a photographer. The photographer and the priest were Indian; the couple and the bridesmaid could have been American or European—it was difficult to tell.

It had been two years, Melissa thought, but she still hadn't got over that initial jolt whenever she saw a blond male in his twenties. The groom wasn't Josh, but for a second she'd thought he was, and her heart-rate had tripled. Even now she couldn't help stopping to look, just to make sure that it wasn't him.

'I don't think we should stare,' Samir

prompted. 'It's a rather private moment, don't you think?'

By then Melissa had got her wits about her, and she managed to retort, 'It's not very private if they've decided to get married on a public beach, is it? It's like deciding to hold a Kuchipudi performance on Flora Fountain and then getting offended if people don't pay for tickets.'

'Kuchipudi? Why Kuchipudi?' Samir was saying in bemused tones when the bridesmaid came running across to them.

'Hey, guys…if you've got a minute…Brenda and Mark just got married, and it'd be lovely if you could come across and share some champagne. Oh, I'm Sarah by the way—so nice to meet you!'

Sarah was definitely American, and from the sound of it had been at the champagne for a while now. It was difficult to refuse the invitation without sounding completely churlish, and Samir shrugged and smiled as they followed her to where the bride was trying to settle down on a plastic chair without completely ruining her dress.

Both she and the groom looked so completely happy that for a second Melissa's breath caught in her throat. This was what *she'd* hoped for once. Mark even looked a bit like Josh—she hadn't been completely delusional in the few seconds when she'd mistaken one for the other.

'He proposed when we were in Agra,' Brenda told them. 'Right in front of the Taj Mahal.'

OK, so it wasn't a very original place to propose, but Melissa couldn't help feeling touched. She took the glass of champagne Sarah was offering her and smiled. 'So getting married in India was a spur-of-the-moment thing?'

'Yes—actually, we've just exchanged vows. There'll be a proper legal ceremony when we go back.'

'So how about you two, then—are you a couple?'

While the question had been addressed to both of them, it was clear by the way Sarah was leaning towards Samir that it was his answer she was interested in.

'No, we just work together,' he said, but already he was drawing back from her, his expression becoming formal and shuttered off. 'We should leave,' he said in an undertone to Melissa.

'Why? You just got here. Have another drink before you go,' Sarah urged.

She'd not taken her eyes off Samir, and Melissa felt a second's atavistic urge to lean across and claw the other woman's eyes out. The impulse didn't last for more than a second, but it left her feeling more than a little shaken. Granted, Samir in his current bare-chested state looked like the answer to every single woman's prayer, but he was still her boss—where had that momentary surge of possessiveness come from? Luckily Samir was too focussed on getting away to notice her temporary confusion.

'D'you want your shirt back?' she couldn't help asking wryly as they got away from a visibly disappointed Sarah. 'I think you're more of a temptation to the opposite sex than I am.'

To her surprise, Samir flushed. 'Is your top dry now?' was all he said.

'Dry enough. I won't get arrested for indecent exposure at least,' she said, pulling his T-shirt off and handing it back to him. They walked on in silence for a bit, and then Melissa said, 'It was rather sweet, wasn't it? Those two deciding to exchange vows on the beach?'

Samir shrugged. 'I give that marriage one year,' he said. 'Proposing at the Taj Mahal, getting married in Goa—its unreal. Once they're back in Chicago and squabbling about who gets to do the washing up they'll come back to earth.' Melissa gave an involuntary little giggle and Samir frowned. 'Something funny?'

'You're like the hero of a romance novel,' she said. 'Tall, brooding and cynical. All you need is a murky past and a scar on your forehead.' Like a romance novel hero, he was also sexy as hell—but she prudently didn't say that.

'Brooding and cynical?'

He sounded thoughtful, and Melissa gave him an apprehensive look, wondering if she'd gone too far.

Evidently not, because after a pause he asked, with genuine curiosity, 'Is that what the heroes in romance novels are like?'

'All of them,' she assured him. 'And they don't believe in love *ever*—until the very last chapter. My neighbour in the hostel is a romance novel junkie—she buys them by the dozen.'

'And you borrow them from her?'

'Sometimes,' Melissa said and laughed. 'No, actually I borrow them often—I'm just trying to pretend that I'm the highbrow type. I used to laugh at the plots at first, but they're actually quite addictive.'

'Right...' Samir said.

His phone pinged and he took it out of his pocket to look at the display.

'Sorry, I need to make some calls. I'll see you later—will you be able to get back to the hotel by yourself?'

A little startled by the abrupt brush-off, Melissa retorted, 'I'll try. I'm sure I can manage to find it.'

He didn't reply, still staring at his phone, and, feeling annoyed and just a little hurt, she marched off towards the hotel.

'It's one long jamboree,' Devdeep said. 'They'll announce the actual awards tomorrow.'

They were at the pre-awards cocktail party, and Melissa had been stuck with Devdeep and another colleague at one end of the room while Samir stood talking to a group from another agency at the other end. Luckily the event was in the same hotel they were booked into—at a pinch she could always develop a killing headache and escape to her room.

Melissa involuntarily looked across at Samir. He looked bored, as if he found the drinking and the locker room jokes tedious and a little immature.

Devdeep followed the direction of her eyes. 'Bit arrogant, isn't he?' he said, evidently expecting Melissa to agree with him. 'Doesn't make the slightest effort to mingle—probably thinks he's way too important to hang with small fry like us.'

'He might just be shy,' she suggested, realising how completely stupid she sounded as soon as the words were out of her mouth. Samir was to shy what Godzilla was to a garden lizard.

'You drove down with him, didn't you? Did you find out anything—his plans for the agency, that kind of stuff? Now that Brian's gone we can really catapult this agency into the big league, as long as Samir is willing to invest in it.' At her blank look, Devdeep's eyebrows flew up. 'You didn't ask him a thing? God, I wish I'd known he was driving you here; I'd have briefed you properly. What *did* you talk about, then?'

Bougainvillaea, she felt like saying. *And whether Kolhapuri* chappals *were invented in Kolhapur.*

'We...um...didn't talk much,' she said instead. 'He was concentrating on the road.'

Shivani, the other colleague with them, intervened. 'Devdeep, you're such a nerd,' she said. 'The guy's super-hot—I'm sure Melissa had better things to talk to him about than your stupid plans for world domination.'

At that point Samir looked across and caught Melissa's eye. Immediately, she felt her face grow warm, though she knew he couldn't have heard a word of their conversation.

'You're blushing,' Shivani said with satisfaction. 'Which means I'm right.'

'Nonsense,' Melissa retorted, but by now her ears were burning with embarrassment. 'Besides, he's way out of my league.'

'Yes, of course,' Devdeep said, evidently under the impression that he was rescuing Melissa from an uncomfortable conversation. 'Look at him—he's rich and good-looking. He could date anyone he wants!'

'Thanks, Devdeep,' she said drily.

He looked a little taken aback. 'I didn't mean...'

'No, of course you didn't.' She sighed.

Devdeep was right—no one sane would imagine that Samir was the slightest bit interested in her. And with all the dumb things she'd said about romantic novels he would probably avoid her as if she was the latest variant in bird flu.

Getting up, she said, 'I think I'll take a stroll outside. I need some fresh air—this place stinks of cigarette smoke.'

Once outside, she hesitated a little before going up to the reception desk. It was too early to go back to her room, but she didn't fancy hanging around in the lobby all alone—maybe there was a library or somewhere she could hang out until it was time for dinner.

When Samir came out of the bar a few minutes later she was deep in conversation with the concierge, discussing the relative merits of a game of billiards and a visit to the hotel's overpriced gift shop.

Samir stood watching her silently for a few minutes. Utterly unconscious of his presence, she made a charming picture as she politely scanned the list of guided tours that the concierge was thrusting on her. She was wearing a rather demure long-sleeved black dress, but her hair tumbled down her back in loose curls. The only make-up she had on was lip gloss and kohl around her eyes. The kohl emphasised the doe-like beauty of her brown eyes, and her mouth was pink and lush.

For a few seconds Samir imagined pressing his own lips onto hers. Then he came to his senses with a jerk. He'd followed her out to apologise for his earlier brusqueness at the beach, and he'd intended to say his piece and go back to the party. Standing by and gazing at her like a lust-ridden college kid was so far off the agenda it wasn't funny.

Melissa turned just then and caught sight of him, a lovely smile breaking out across her face. At the same moment, Samir noticed that the deceptively demure dress had a plunging neckline, and his already racing pulse-rate responded excitedly.

'I've been driving these people crazy,' she remarked *sotto voce* as she came up to him. 'They can't deal with anyone who doesn't want to go to the spa or go sightseeing.'

Samir was about to reply when he realised that Melissa had gone very still, staring at a man who had just entered the lobby.

The man was dark-skinned and in his late twenties, and he was staring back at Melissa as if he couldn't believe his eyes. Then, in a few quick steps, he crossed to her and grabbed her wrist, barking out something in Konkani. Samir whirled around, but something in Melissa's expression stopped him from intervening.

'What are you doing here?' the man demanded, almost shaking Melissa. 'And who's the guy?'

'My boss,' she said. 'Let me go, *men*, you're making a scene.'

Her Goan accent had suddenly become more pronounced, and her eyes were flashing with rage. As soon as she said the magic 'boss' word, though, the man released her arm, looking embarrassed.

Melissa sighed.

'Samir, meet my brother Michael,' she said. Then she elbowed Michael and said a few rapid sentences in Konkani. Probably something like, *Stop being a boor and be polite to my scary boss or he'll sack me*, because Michael held out a hand to Samir with a passable imitation of a polite smile.

'Welcome to Goa, *men*,' he said. 'Are you here for work?'

'No, he's here to look at the coconut trees,' Melissa said tartly. 'Of course we're here for work. How are Cheryl and the kids?'

'They're fine,' he said awkwardly. 'Justin still talks about you—asks about his Melly Aunty.'

He didn't look angry any longer, Samir noted—just upset and confused. Evidently there was a lot wrong here.

'And how's…' Melissa didn't complete the sentence, but Michael understood her.

'Dad's fine,' he said. 'Though his blood pressure's been on the high side. Come and see him, Melissa. It's been such a long while…. I can't believe you're here in Goa and didn't even tell me.'

It was clear that Melissa didn't want to reply,

and Samir came to the rescue. 'We should be joining the others,' he said in what he hoped was a suitably authoritative tone. 'Maybe you could catch up with your brother some time tomorrow, Melissa?'

Michael looked as if he wanted to say something, but he didn't get a chance—Melissa gave him a hug and said, 'He's right. There's heaps of things to do—mustn't dawdle. I'll call you, Mickey *dada*. Sorry, Samir.'

Samir took the cue, and after giving Michael a quick nod turned and strode away towards the hotel lobby. Melissa scurried after him, and after a few minutes he shortened his stride so that she could keep up.

'Thanks,' she said as they entered the hotel.

Michael was still standing where they had left him, his expression puzzled and a little hurt, and Melissa was feeling dreadfully guilty. Not guilty enough to go back and have a proper conversation with him, but enough to want to be out of his sight.

Samir looked around. It was only seven, and

there was an hour before dinner started. 'Do you want to go and wait in the bar till dinner begins, or would you like to go back to your room?'

'Bar,' Melissa said gloomily. 'Though I won't be very good company. I wish I drank. I'd like to get completely sloshed.'

She looked so ruffled that Samir impulsively put an arm around her and gave her an affectionate squeeze.

It was a perfectly innocuous gesture—brotherly, even—Melissa could only blame her own overactive hormones for her instant reaction. Trying not to be obvious by pulling away abruptly, she stayed absolutely still until he let go of her.

Seemingly unconscious of the upheaval he'd caused in her mind, he asked, 'Family problems?'

'The family has problems with me,' she said. 'So, yes, I suppose you could call it family problems.'

He waited till she was sitting down with a

glass of juice in her hand before he said, 'Want to talk about it?'

'I wouldn't want to bore you,' she said. 'It's not such a big deal.'

But clearly it was—her voice was wobbly and her eyes looked suspiciously damp.

Samir put a hand lightly over hers. 'I don't get bored easily,' he said.

'My dad disowned me a couple of years ago,' she said tightly. 'Struck my name out of the family Bible and all that. Michael was pretty upset with me as well, but he's come around. Cheryl's level-headed—she must have talked some sense into him.'

'What happened—a guy?'

Melissa grimaced. 'Predictable, isn't it? My dad flipped out. It wasn't even anything terribly serious—just a teenage crush—I'd have lost interest if he hadn't made such a fuss.'

Samir frowned. Something didn't sound quite right. 'He threw you out of the house because you had a crush on a guy?'

'No…not exactly. I was going through a rebellious phase, and… Well, I overstepped the mark quite a bit. Anyway, let's talk about something else; my love life isn't exactly the most thrilling topic.'

'Neither is mine,' Samir said, his voice deadpan. 'So that leaves politics and the economy. At this rate we'll soon be reduced to talking about the weather.'

In spite of herself, Melissa laughed. 'Storms are brewing in North Goa,' she said. 'That's where my folks live.'

'What was he like?' Samir asked abruptly.

There was something vaguely unsettling in the thought of Melissa having had a relationship serious enough for her to have broken ties with her family. Evidently the man was no longer in the picture—maybe they'd broken up afterwards.

'I don't want to talk about it,' Melissa said, shaking her head firmly. 'I need to take my mind off him, and my brother, and… Oh, what the heck? I think I'll have a drink after all.' She beckoned to a waiter and ordered a vodka with orange juice.

'Are you sure you can handle that?' Samir asked, eyeing the way she glugged it back with misgiving.

Melissa laughed. 'I come from a family of hard drinkers,' she said. 'My grandmother could probably drink you under the table. Turning tee-total was my way of rebelling.'

Many rounds later, Samir had to acknowledge that Melissa had inherited her grandmother's capacity for strong liquor. Not a heavy drinker himself, he was beginning to feel the effect of the vodkas. Melissa, on the other hand, was looking just the same—maybe just a tad more bight-eyed and chatty than she had been at the start of the evening.

'One more?' she asked, tapping Samir's empty glass with her finger.

He shook his head ruefully. 'I'm done,' he said. 'Any more and they'll have to carry me out of here.'

'Bo-ring,' she said. 'Come on, Samir, don't

be a wuss. I was hoping you'd take me dancing after this.'

'Sorry—too old,' he said. 'Why don't you go with that Akash guy who was trying to chat you up so desperately?'

'Ah, so you noticed?' Melissa said. 'He's cute, but he's not really my type. Too chirpy. I like cynical brooding types.'

She was giving him a frankly assessing look, and Samir wondered if he'd got his initial reading wrong. Maybe she *was* drunk after all. Whatever the reason, the way she was looking at him was enough to make any red-blooded male lose his head.

Hurriedly, he got to his feet, reminding himself why he couldn't touch her. She was young, probably drunk, and she was an employee— there was no way he could pull her into his arms and kiss her senseless the way he wanted to. Better to leave before things got out of hand.

'I'm going to bed,' he said when she gave him an inquiring look.

'Ooh, good idea,' she said, sliding off the bar stool. 'I'll come with you.'

All right, so she was definitely drunk. For a few seconds he thought he'd heard her wrong. Then he thought he'd misunderstood—but clearly he hadn't.

'Melissa,' he said as she followed him down the winding path that led to his cottage. 'Your room's the other way; it's in the main part of the hotel.'

'Of course it is,' she said, laughing at him. 'But I'm not going there. I'm coming with you.'

She was feeling reckless—a combination of alcohol and the euphoria of being back in Goa. It had also been a long while since her last relationship had broken up. In the dim light of the bar Samir looked every inch a sex god, and resisting temptation seemed downright stupid.

'Look, I don't think this is a good idea,' he said. 'We've both had too much to drink, and...'

'And we shouldn't do something we'll regret tomorrow?' Melissa wrinkled her nose. 'Samir, if you wrote your own ads they'd be so full of clichés you'd have to pay copyright to the greetings cards company.'

'Melissa…'

'Shh,' she said and, leaning up, she kissed him full on the mouth.

Her lips were inviting, warm and lush against his, and then there was her pliant body, pressed provocatively against his. Involuntarily, Samir found himself returning the kiss, his arms coming up to pull her closer.

They were almost at the cottage, and later he couldn't remember opening the door or switching on the lights. But he did remember carrying her to bed and undressing her. And drinking in the sight of her near perfect body spread out on the bed before making wild, passionate love to her all night long.

CHAPTER FOUR

'AND THE AWARD for the best copy goes to…'

There was a long pause, and Melissa thought she'd keel over and die if they gave it to someone else.

'Mendonca Advertising for their groundbreaking, story format ad for India's most popular brand of baby soap. Come on, let's hear it for them!'

The hall burst into applause as Samir went on stage to accept the award. 'I know this isn't the Oscars, so I'll keep it short,' he said, smiling around at the audience.

Melissa noticed that several of the women immediately sat up and began preening.

'I've taken over at Mendonca Advertising only very recently. The people who really deserve the award are Brian Mendonca, the man who set up the firm, Devdeep Dutta, for a superb pitch that got us the account, but most of all Melissa D'Cruz, the talented young copy-writer who wrote the ad for us.'

The applause wasn't overwhelming, exactly, but it was loud, and it went on till Melissa and Devdeep had accepted the award and returned to their seats.

'Nice of him to mention Brian,' Devdeep said in an undertone.

'He could hardly *not* mention Brian,' Melissa said tartly. 'The agency still carries his name. Anyway, the ad was done long before Samir arrived on the scene.'

'Congrats, guys,' Samir said, coming to stand next to them. 'Very well deserved.'

Melissa gave a polite smile, pretending not to be affected by his nearness. She'd sneaked out of his room early in the morning before he woke up, and had spent the rest of the day avoiding him. There was the awkwardness, of course, of having practically thrown herself at him—her seduction skills were pathetic, and she hadn't even had the excuse of being properly drunk…

not that it had seemed to matter to Samir...he'd responded pretty enthusiastically—but it wasn't just awkwardness. It was also that he was her boss, and one-night stands were sensible only if you were never going to see the person again.

He was looking at her now, and Melissa flushed automatically. The previous night had been...memorable. Samir was phenomenal in bed, and she'd been pretty vocal with her appreciation. So vocal that the memory of some of the things she'd said was making her cringe in embarrassment now. He probably thought she was a complete slut.

'You left,' he said in a low voice, once Devdeep had moved off. 'Why? I tried calling you, but your phone was switched off and you weren't in your room.'

'I went parasailing,' she said. 'My phone was in my room.'

'Parasailing?' he said thoughtfully. 'That's a new one. I don't think anyone's used *that* as an excuse to walk out on me before. Was I that bad?'

He seemed more amused than angry, and Melissa felt a rush of relief. 'You were spectacular, and you know it,' she said frankly. 'It's just that I thought I'd save us both an awkward morning-after.'

Samir reached out and touched her face lightly, and she felt her body automatically quiver with longing.

'I'd have preferred it if you'd stayed,' he said.

The simple statement went a long way towards calming her down.

'I wasn't sure,' she said. 'This isn't the kind of thing I do normally. I was in a bit of a reckless mood after meeting Michael, and I thought a one-night stand would be a good way to take my mind off things. Well, it worked!' she added defensively at the incredulous look in his face.

'Happy to help,' he said drily. 'Why did you do a runner, then?'

'You're my boss. Sleeping with the boss is never a good idea. I kind of forgot that bit in the heat of the moment last night.'

Samir stayed silent. He'd expected her to be

shaken up, even embarrassed. Being told that he'd been a temporary diversion to take her mind off her more serious problems was a bit of a facer.

As if she'd read his mind, Melissa said, 'I don't make a habit of this. Yesterday was a bit of an aberration.'

'An aberration you don't want to repeat?'

'Um, yes. I mean, no, I don't want to repeat it. It was great, but it'll only become awkward with me working for you. People would figure it out and think I was sleeping with you to boost my career.'

OK, this was coming out all wrong, and Samir was looking clearly irritated, his per-fectly sculpted mouth tightening with annoy-ance. And staring at his mouth was making her think of all the things that very same mouth had done last night, and she was going all hot and cold at the memory.

'You have a point,' he was saying now. 'Your career could do with a bit of a boost—being a copywriter with a tiny ad agency can't be where your ambitions end, can it?'

Melissa's eyes widened. Granted, his ego must have taken a bit of a beating when she'd told him that she didn't want to sleep with him again, but he was being insulting now.

'Look, there's no need to turn nasty,' she said, getting to her feet. 'I'm flattered that you think I'm ambitious enough to sleep with you because you're a big dude in the advertising world, but it isn't true. I slept with you because you've got a good body and sexy eyes, and ever since I met you I've been wondering what you'd be like in bed. Best way to get you out of my system.'

She put her rather cute little nose in the air and walked off before Samir could think of a suitable response.

Staring after her, he was surprised to find himself laughing. He'd never been put so firmly in his place before, and he found his respect for Melissa going up several notches. He'd re-acted stupidly when she'd come out with that line about boosting her career, but it had trig-

gered off a set of memories that he'd spent the
last ten years trying to bury. Definitely not her
fault, and he'd apologise as soon as he possibly could.

The one thing he knew was that he'd make
sure he was more than a simple one-night stand
for Melissa—she was worth fighting for.

Melissa's heart was pounding rather hard as
she walked to the other end of the poolside garden where the award ceremony was being held.
Her little outburst at Samir might mean that
she'd shortly be out of a job, but she found she
didn't care about that as much as she did about
the thought of not seeing him again. She'd been
lying about having got Samir out of her system—if anything, that one night with him had
left her wanting far, far more.

A vaguely familiar-looking group of people
near the bar smiled at her—with some effort
she recognised her cricket teammates from the
previous day's game on the beach.

Akash was waving to her. 'Congratulations,'
he said, coming up to her and giving her an ex-

travagant hug. 'I was trying to get your attention earlier, but you were completely engrossed in whatever Mr Razdan was saying to you. I do hope you managed to swing a better salary—you deserve it.'

For one horrified moment Melissa thought he meant that she deserved a higher salary for having slept with her boss. Then she realised he meant the award, and said, 'It didn't occur to me to ask for more money.'

'You should ask him now. There are a dozen other agencies here who'd hire you on the spot at double the pay. Actually, my boss has already been asking about you.' He gave her an engaging grin. 'She comes to these award dos to sniff out the talent. Saves her having to pay a headhunter. Interested?'

'What's she like to work for?'

Akash shrugged. 'A bit hormonal. Fundamentally OK, though. And you'd have brilliant colleagues like me to work with if you joined.'

Oh, dear—she'd really have to figure out a way of telling Akash she wasn't interested. The cricket game on the beach seemed to have given him all kinds of ideas.

She was trying to think of a polite way of giving him the brush-off when she saw his gaze shift to over her shoulder.

'The guy doesn't leave you alone for a minute, does he?' Akash muttered. He scribbled something on the back of a napkin and thrust it at her. 'Here—call me once Svengali's gone. I'll set up something with Maya.'

'New conquest?' Samir asked, once Akash was gone. 'Or is he launching a takeaway service?'

'Funny joke,' Melissa said, wrinkling up her nose. 'Not. He was offering me a job.'

Samir didn't seem to have heard what she'd said, and Melissa began to feel a little annoyed. Okay, maybe she wasn't in the big league, exactly, but it was pretty flattering being head-hunted by someone as well known as Maya Kumar.

She'd recognised the name the second Akash had mentioned it. Maya was a legend in Indian advertising circles, having quit as the creative director of a multinational advertising firm to set up her own company. Ten years later she was running one of India's most successful agencies, and Melissa found the thought of working for her rather exciting.

'I came to check if you'd like to go out for dinner,' Samir was saying. 'Unless, of course, you've already made other plans?'

'I have,' she said shortly, and added, as his eyes automatically shifted to where Akash was standing with a group of friends, 'I'm meeting Michael and Cheryl. Thought it was time to try and do some patching up.' There had been no real need to tell him that, but she'd hate him to think that she'd jump straight out of his bed into a flirtation with another man.

He looked surprised. 'You sure about this? I thought you wanted to avoid your brother.'

'I can't avoid him for the rest of my life. And I really want to see my nephew.'

'I can drop you,' Samir offered. 'Wherever

you're meeting them. And hang around if you need moral support.'

He really seemed to have missed the point of a one-night stand, Melissa thought in exasperation. Moral support was *so* not part of the deal. It didn't help that he was looking especially hot today, in a tailored jacket worn over an open-necked shirt and jeans that fitted his long legs and lean thighs like a second skin. Nor that the hotel had quoted her a perfectly outrageous rate for a cab to Panaji, where she was meeting Michael. A week's salary for a ride in a smelly old cab versus a *gratis* trip to Panaji and back in Samir's top-of-the-range roadster—she could be forgiven for giving in. Still, it was better to make some things clear.

'What I said earlier, about getting you out of my system...'

'You meant it. I know. And I'm sorry I said what I did—put it down to my ego not being used to a bruising.' He gave her a quick smile. 'We'll stick to being just good friends, OK?'

Impossible to tell whether he was serious or

not, but Melissa decided she didn't care. It was only by exercising super-human self-control that she was sticking to her self-imposed no touching policy with Samir. There was no point inflicting further torture on herself by refusing a simple lift.

'Let's go, then,' she said, giving him a sunny smile in return.

They were halfway to Panaji, and Melissa was just beginning to relax, when Samir spoke.

'Are you meeting your father as well? Or just your brother's family?'

'Just my brother,' Melissa said and sighed. 'I don't think I'm up to the strain of meeting my dad just yet.'

'He seems quite a tyrant. What does he do?'

'He owns a restaurant in North Goa,' she said. 'We all used to chip in: my mom, me, Michael and Cheryl—even my nephew used to hang around there the whole day. And when I finished college I started working there full-time. My dad was getting older, and we'd expanded a bit—he needed all the help he could get.'

Samir shot her a quick look. She sounded wistful, and a little sad, as if she wasn't quite as blasé about being cut off from her family as she pretended to be.

'Your mother?'

'She died six years ago,' Melissa said.

The words were matter-of-fact, but he could tell she was not over it yet.

'A road accident.'

'I'm sorry,' Samir said.

Melissa shrugged. 'It was quick—that was a mercy. She didn't suffer much.'

Unlike her family, Samir thought, trying to imagine how tough it would have been for Melissa, losing her mother while still in her teens. She was staring out of the window unseeingly now, and he swiftly steered the conversation so that she started talking about her nephew. That cheered her up almost instantly, and by the time he dropped her off at Panaji, she was smiling again.

He was deep in thought as he drove towards the waterfront. The Mandovi River passed right by Panaji, and after he'd parked the car he found a little restaurant that overlooked it. It was the first time in a long, long while that he'd been involved enough with a woman to worry about her. Not used to analysing his own feelings, he tried to tell himself that it was the natural result of the rushed relationship they'd had. One day they'd hardly known each other, the next they were having wild, passionate sex. And now they were acting out a 'just friends' charade that was a positive insult to his status as a red-blooded male.

Samir's phone rang when he was halfway through his dessert.

'Can you come and pick me up?' a quiet voice asked.

Immediately he knew something was wrong.

'Where?' he asked, and she named a popular store on the main street.

'I'm standing outside,' she said.

She looked positively woebegone when he drew up in front of her.

'Everything OK?' he asked gently, seeing how close to tears she was.

'Justin didn't recognise me,' she said. 'My own nephew. And Michael didn't tell him who I was because he was worried he'd go home and tell Dad. They sneaked out to meet me like I'm some kind of fallen woman or something. Michael kept saying that I should go and meet our parish priest—apparently he's the only person Dad discusses me with.'

She was practically shaking with rage, and once they were out of the tiny city Samir pulled up to the side and held out his arms. Melissa glared at him for a few seconds, as if he was personally responsible for the mess her life was in. Then, with a half suppressed sob, she crept into his arms.

Her body was soft and yielding against his, and because she wasn't crying any longer, just holding on to him for comfort, he felt no guilt in tipping up her face after a few minutes and kissing her. He'd meant the kiss to be gentle, but she seemed to go up in flames as soon as his lips touched hers.

'Hey...' he said softly as her fingers fumbled

eagerly at his shirt buttons. 'Maybe we should get back to the hotel.'

For a few seconds she didn't seem to have heard him, and then she gave a shaky little laugh and drew away from him. 'You're right,' she agreed. 'Before the morality police catch up with us.'

She didn't say anything about having got him out of her system, he noted with satisfaction as he started the car.

'You're the first man I've been with after Josh,' Melissa said abruptly after a few minutes.

Samir glanced across at her. He'd thought as much after the previous night—she wasn't in-experienced, exactly, but it was evident that she didn't sleep around. Why she would want to give the impression that she did was something else altogether.

'So the one-night stand thing…?'

'Was just me trying to prove to myself that I could do casual sex if I wanted to.' She made a funny little grimace. 'Didn't work.'

Samir couldn't help laughing at her expression. 'You know what? I'm glad it didn't,' he said. 'At the risk of sounding impossibly old-fashioned, I must admit that I don't really approve of casual sex. And I'd like us to be more than a one-night stand.'

Melissa wrinkled her nose. 'What? Like a proper relationship?'

'Something like that.' They had stopped at a traffic light, and he leaned across and kissed her bare shoulder, making her shiver in reaction. 'Don't think about it right now, though.'

The light changed, and they were moving again, so Melissa didn't ask why not. Instead, she asked, 'Were you in a relationship before this?'

The way she said 'relationship' was incredibly cute—rather like a precocious child trying out a new word—and Samir smiled involuntarily. It was one of the most attractive things about Melissa: the little flashes of naiveté that showed between the chinks of her self-assured, woman-in-charge-of-her-own-sexuality persona.

'Not a serious one,' he said. 'But I was dating someone for almost year.'

Her eyebrows flew up. 'You spent a *year* with someone you weren't serious about?'

He shrugged. 'We thought it would work out initially. And it was convenient to have someone to bring along to social dos.'

'It sounds awful,' Melissa said frankly. 'And before that?'

'Before that I had a very intense fling with a journalist. That time we were both clear it wasn't going to last.'

'You're an even bigger disaster than I am,' Melissa said. 'The L word didn't happen ever? Even when you were in college?'

He was silent for a few seconds, and then he said, 'It did happen. Not when I was in college, but very soon after I graduated. Turns out I picked the wrong person.'

'She met someone else?'

He shook his head. 'No, just changed her mind about me. But it was a long while ago. Tell me about the guy you were with—why was your father so against him?'

As soon as the words were out of his mouth he wished he hadn't asked. Her face clouded over again, and she bit her lip.

'Josh was Australian—that was one thing. And he was definitely not serious about me; it was just a holiday romance as far as he was concerned.'

Samir hesitated a little. He'd shifted the conversation away from his own botched-up love life because he hated talking about the one period in his life when he'd let another person control him emotionally. He hadn't, however, wanted to make Melissa relive what had probably been a more traumatic experience—in his case at least his family had been kept out of it. Now he could hardly change the topic again without seeming callous, so he searched around for a question that would show he was listening without being overly intrusive.

'How did you meet Josh?' he asked finally.

'He came into the restaurant when I was doing

the lunch shift. He was a travel writer, and he was in Goa to do some background research for his new book. I was used to foreigners—our restaurant had got good reviews on quite a few travel websites and we got dozens of tourists coming in every day. Josh was different. He'd been in the country only for a few weeks, but he seemed totally at home—like he was born here. We got talking, and…well, before I knew it I'd agreed to help him out with his research. I speak Konkani, and even a little Portuguese, and he needed someone to translate when he interviewed the locals.'

Samir felt a totally alien emotion sweep over him—it took him a few seconds to realise that it was jealousy. Melissa's voice had taken on a wistful tone that he'd never heard before, and he had a mad urge to hunt Josh down and smash his face in for him. Because he'd quite obviously hurt Melissa—not to mention messing up her relationship with her family.

It took some effort keeping his voice neutral

as he asked, 'Your father didn't stop you from dating him?'

'He didn't know for a long while,' Melissa said. 'Josh used to flirt with me a little, but I didn't take it seriously at first. Then we started spending more time together—he showed me the work he'd already done on the book, and it was amazing. He wrote really well. You could visualise each sentence. I think I fell for his writing first. My dad found out I was having an affair with Josh just a week before he was due to leave India. I didn't want to miss those last few days with him and I refused to listen to my dad. Just packed up a bag and moved into Josh's place. He'd paid the rent for a full quarter, so after he left I had a place to stay for a while. My dad refused to let me into the house.'

'How did you end up in Mumbai, then?'

'I called Aunty Liz. She's Brian's wife, and she's a kind of cousin several times removed. I've always been close to her, and I thought she could help me get a job outside Goa. I majored in English literature—it's a pretty useless qualification, but I write pretty well. Brian offered me a copywriting job, and it seemed like the perfect solution.'

'Are you still in touch with him?'

'With Brian?' Melissa asked, looking puzzled. For an instant, Samir felt like shaking her.

'Oh, you mean Josh. Well, yes—he e-mails me sometimes, but we're just friends now. I'm over him, if that's what you're asking.'

It was exactly what he was asking, and the casual way in which she said she was over Josh was more believable than if she'd protested vehemently.

'I don't know if I was really in love with him either,' she said after a while. 'It was all so mixed up. I didn't mind working in the restaurant, but a part of me had always wanted to escape. Then there was something glamorous about dating a foreigner—especially a writer. Maybe I just got a little carried away, trying to prove that I was an independent woman with a life of my own.' There was another little pause, and then she said, 'Or at least that's what I tell myself now. At the time I was pretty besotted with him. I even hoped he'd take me with him when he left India.'

'You were pretty young,' Samir said easily. 'Most people get carried away the first time they fall in love.'

'I guess,' Melissa said, adding silently to herself that 'most people', however, didn't run away from their families—or ignore the opposite sex for two years after the relationship ended and then suddenly decide that they wanted to have a casual relationship with the first man they found attractive.

Twisting her hands together in her lap, Melissa felt suddenly very close to tears. She'd thought she'd moved on—become a different person from the confused, heart-sore and rebellious girl who'd left Goa two years ago. Meeting Michael and Cheryl had brought it all back, and she didn't feel anywhere near as confident about her choices as she had earlier.

Especially after Michael had put a hand over hers and said, in his quiet way, 'Dadda and me didn't behave right with you, Melly. You'd never have left us if Mamma was still there.'

He was right, and that made it all so much worse. She'd whisked her hand out from under his and announced tightly that she needed to leave. Then she'd called Samir, wanting—no, *needing* his quiet strength by her side. And he'd been wonderful, encouraging her to talk without prying unnecessarily or turning judgemental. Not in the least like Josh, who'd hated any kind of emotional outburst—especially when it had to do with her family.

They were at the hotel now, and Samir pulled into the parking lot. Immediately the atmosphere between them changed, and Melissa felt a shiver of anticipation run through her. Samir came around to open her door and she automatically went into his arms as soon as she got out of the car. It felt like coming home as she inhaled the now familiar smell of his aftershave and pressed even closer to his hard, muscular body.

He was perfect, she thought as a wave of lust

swept over her. Strong and gentle and wildly exciting all at the same time—she'd been crazy to think that a single night with him would be enough.

The kiss was slow this time, and unexpectedly sensuous, and when his lips finally left hers Melissa found herself clinging on to him for support.

A little breathlessly, she asked, 'Your room or mine?'

CHAPTER FIVE

'MOVE IN WITH YOU?' Melissa looked a little taken aback. 'Isn't that a bit drastic? We only met a couple of weeks ago.'

'It's the practical thing to do,' Samir said. 'I'm at serious risk of dying of frustration.'

It was a week since they'd returned from Goa, and they'd managed to spend only one afternoon together. Melissa's hostel had a curfew, and Samir was working crazy hours as he tried to get Mendonca's finances into shape before he handed it over to a new business head and moved back to Maximus. Sure, they saw each other in the office, but that wasn't enough—after spending their last few days in Goa almost exclusively in bed, it was torture having to pretend that they were just colleagues.

The thought of actually going back to the same house and sleeping—or staying awake—

in the same bed was so incredibly tempting that the practicalities didn't strike Melissa for several minutes.

'What if it doesn't work out?' she asked. 'We might get tired of each other, or you might find out that I'm such a slob you can't bear having me around in your house.' Another thought occurred to her, and she went on without giving him a chance to interrupt. 'I'd have to give up my room in the hostel. There's no way I'll get it back later.'

'You won't need it later,' Samir said. 'Look, let's give it a shot. If it works—great. If not, we'll part ways, and I swear I'll help you find a place to live that's even better than your too-good-to-be-true hostel. I want us to be together.'

He was leaning forward a little as he spoke, and although his words were ordinary enough Melissa felt an automatic little thrill run through her in response to the simmering desire in his eyes.

'What about people at the agency finding out?'

Samir shrugged. 'Half of them have already

guessed,' he said. 'And the rest don't need to know anything other than that you're my girl-friend.'

He was right, and the only reason Melissa still hesitated was because she knew that she was getting into murky waters here. A quick, no-holds-barred fling was what she'd wanted. But, like the lady in her favourite washing powder ad, she'd got a lot more than she'd expected. A heartbreakingly good-looking boyfriend. A complicated decision to make.

Sneaking a quick look at Samir, she won-dered why it felt so tough. Sure, Brian and Liz would probably be horrified if she moved in with Samir, but her other friends wouldn't care much. It was more that she herself wasn't sure it was the right thing to do.

Perhaps if she'd met him a few years later she'd have been panting to move in with him. But right now her plans included rising up the agency ranks to make creative director, writing the perfect novel and travelling around India in her spare time. By train, because she was still flight-phobic. Men figured in her plans, but in the relative scheme of things they were at the same level of importance as the ad breaks on a movie channel.

Samir, however, showed signs of wanting to be the main feature film—worse, if she didn't get a grip on her life that was exactly what he'd end up being. It wasn't that she didn't like him. She did—a lot. But falling for him would clearly be a bad idea. He moved in completely different circles from her—his friends were socialites and high-flying executives, and Melissa knew she'd feel deeply uncomfortable with them.

Also, his lifestyle was as different from hers as a Bollywood star's was from the man who ran the corner *vada-pav* stall. He'd never commuted by bus or local train, and he'd looked surprised and a little disbelieving when she'd told him that she actually preferred public transport to whizzing around in an air-conditioned car. And he hated eating out at the little roadside joints she favoured. Small things, but they all added up to make the practical side of her brain think that their living together might not be idyllic. In spite of the red-hot sex.

Then again, the practical side of her brain hadn't had much of a say in the decisions she'd made since she'd met Samir.

It was difficult thinking things through while Samir was still watching her, his expression inscrutable. Probably he thought she was a right ninny, dithering around instead of saying anything. Wishing she was the organised type—the kind of person who could draw up a mental list of pros and cons and decide in a minute—she frowned as she tried to concentrate.

What other people thought didn't really matter. Nor did it really matter whether she liked his friends or he liked hers. What mattered was whether she wanted to move in with him or not. And the more time she spent with Samir, the more she felt she wanted to.

It wasn't just that he was spectacular in bed— the more she got to know him, the more she liked him as a human being. His aloof, sometimes overly serious work persona concealed a genuinely warm, fun side that she'd got to know over the past couple of weeks. And, unlike Josh, he seemed to be as keen on her as she was about him. She couldn't help the warning bells that went off in her head every time she found herself getting a bit more involved with Samir, but she could decide to ignore them.

'Don't over-think it,' he was saying softly now, his hand moving persuasively up her thigh. 'Just go with the flow.'

God, she'd always hated that expression, but when Samir said it, it sounded positively enticing. Not to mention the way his hand was making her feel. *Impulsive* and *wanton* were the words that came to mind as she said, 'When should I start moving my stuff?'

'Maya Kumar's offered me a job,' Melissa announced two weeks later.

Samir looked up from his computer and frowned. 'The one that guy was speaking to you about? Ashish, or whatever his name was.'

'Akash,' Melissa said. 'Yes, that one. She's

giving me a sixty percent pay-hike and she's also given me the option of working from home. What d'you think?'

'It's your decision,' Samir said slowly. 'Sixty percent is good, but we'd be able to match that here. And I'll be out of Mendonca and on to my next project in a few months—do you still want to leave?'

Melissa plonked herself into the chair opposite Samir. 'We've talked about this,' she said. 'It'll look really weird, you giving me a pay-hike when everyone knows I'm your girlfriend.'

She'd moved into Samir's plush flat a week ago, giving the agency staff enough food for gossip for the next year at least. Other than Dubeyji, the elderly Hindi copywriter, no one had openly expressed disapproval, though Devdeep had taken to addressing her in a terribly stiff and formal way.

Samir shrugged. 'I don't particularly care what they think,' he said.

'Neither do I,' Melissa said honestly. 'But I'd

feel much better getting a raise by changing jobs than…'

'Than sleeping with the boss,' Samir said in resigned tones. 'I know. You've mentioned it a few dozen times already. Go ahead, then.'

Melissa hesitated a little. In the office they tried to keep their conversations as formal as possible, and she wasn't sure if her next question was strictly professional. 'Are you upset with me?' she ventured finally.

Samir looked genuinely surprised. 'No, of course not,' he said. 'You're excellent at your work, and you've got a better offer at a better firm—it's natural you'd want to move.' He glanced at his watch. 'I have a meeting in Bandra—need to rush. Should I leave the car for you?'

'No, I'll take the bus,' Melissa said absently. 'Or, actually, if you're going to be home late I'll go visit Brian and Liz.'

'Keep the car and driver with you, then,' Samir said as he got to his feet. 'I'll ask Kash to book me a cab.'

Melissa knew better than to argue—Samir genuinely didn't get that she preferred walking or public transport to being driven around in his car. It was one of the many things they didn't agree on, and she hadn't got around to talking to him about it. Which would be because she'd spent every spare moment these past two weeks in bed, having wild, delicious sex with Samir—talking hadn't really figured very high on the agenda.

Her mouth automatically curved up at the corners at the thought, and Samir gave her an inquiring look.

'Planning something devilish?' he asked. 'I don't trust you an inch when you get that look in your eyes.'

'I'll tell you when you get home,' she said saucily. 'Off you go to your meeting now.'

She was terribly tempted to lean across and kiss him—he was near enough for her to smell the woody scent of his aftershave, and it could make her go dizzy with longing if she let it.

That was one of her reasons for quitting, she

told herself. It was difficult staying focussed on work when he was around. Only once he was out of the room and she'd gone back to her desk she had to admit to herself that it wasn't the only reason. Nor even the main one. Maya Kumar was very different from Brian, but she had one big thing in common with him—she valued Melissa's work.

Melissa tried to imagine Brian's reaction if she'd quit when he was in charge. He'd have used every trick in the book to hold her back, and he'd have succeeded because she'd have known he wanted her to stay. But Brian had retired, and Samir didn't really care about the agency.

Sighing, Melissa opened up her laptop and began typing out her resignation.

Liz had insisted that she stay for dinner, and it was almost ten when Melissa got back to Samir's apartment complex. It was a tall building in central Mumbai, and he had a massive three-bedroom flat that took up all of one floor—even the bathrooms were larger than the hostel room that Melissa had been living in for the past year. In spite of the scale, the flat had an impersonal look about it, as if it had been designed by an interior decorator as a showcase bachelor pad rather than an actual home.

Samir was still in his office clothes, and he was poring over a sheaf of papers heaped up on the dining table.

'Still working?' Melissa asked, and he leaned back in his chair, running a tanned hand through his already rumpled hair. His jaw was covered with stubble, and he managed to look unkempt and incredibly hot at the same time.

'There's a new deal coming up,' he said. 'A small media company that we might pick up a stake in.'

She crossed the room to him and put her hands on his shoulders. His body was warm and strong under her hands, the muscles flexing as he stretched. Unbidden, her hands started straying over his body—until he pulled away and said, 'I'll finish this in half an hour and be with you, okay?'

Somehow even the dismissal sounded like an invitation, because his dark eyes were dancing wickedly up at her.

'Did you have dinner?' she asked primly, and he shook his head.

'Kamala's son isn't well, apparently—she left a message with the security guard. I'll grab some fruit and cereal in a bit.'

'When?' Melissa asked in disbelief. 'It's ten o'clock. And no one eats fruit and cereal for dinner. Unless they're ill or on a totally weird diet.'

Kamala was the cook, and usually as punctual as clockwork—Samir was clearly incapable of managing without her.

He was still absorbed in work, and all he said was, 'I'm used to eating late. Don't worry about it.'

Melissa wrinkled her nose as she left the room. It was unlikely Samir would eat at all— and going by the last two times he'd brought work home it would be midnight before he came to bed. She gave her reflection in the mirror a rueful look. She'd spent a frantic few minutes in the car fluffing up her hair and redoing her make-up. Pretty much a wasted effort, as Samir hadn't even looked at her properly.

For a mad moment she considered changing into something skimpy and trying to vamp him into bed. Mentally, she reviewed her night wardrobe—teddy bear pyjamas, two striped nighties and a pair of exercise shorts that she normally paired with a tattered T-shirt. Hmm… not much scope for seduction there. Besides, she wasn't sure she had the required *oomph* for a grand seduction scene, even if she'd possessed a suitably titillating wardrobe. She'd lucked out with Samir that first time in Goa, but after that he'd handled all the seducing that needed to be done.

Regretfully giving up the plan, Melissa wandered into the kitchen. Perhaps cooking the poor man dinner was a better idea, she thought, opening the fridge and peering inside. There was very little food in it—from what Melissa could figure Samir's cook bought just enough for two or three meals at a time. Whipping up a cordon bleu meal with two tomatoes, a handful of droopy beans and a capsicum would be next to impossible. Oh, well, Samir would have to manage with a simple pasta dish instead.

Luckily the freezer yielded a pack of frozen chicken, and there was a jar of olives at the back of the store cupboard. Suspiciously turning it around to check the expiry date, Melissa was relieved to find that it was a year away.

She found herself humming under her breath as she put a pot of water on to boil and started chopping the vegetables. One of the things she'd missed most in the hostel was access to a proper kitchen—after so many years of working in her father's restaurant she was a more than competent cook. Samir's kitchen might be poorly stocked, but the equipment was state-of-the-art. The interior designer had evidently pictured Samir in celebrity chef mode—actually, the more Melissa thought about it, Samir in a chef's hat and an apron would look pretty hot.

'What on earth are you doing?' Samir asked, appearing quite suddenly at the door.

Melissa gave a little yelp of alarm, almost dropping the pot of boiling pasta on the ground. 'You startled me!' she said once she'd safely drained the pasta and put the pot in the sink. 'Didn't anyone teach you not to creep up on people like that?'

'I wasn't expecting you to be here,' Samir said, frowning. 'What's that stuff?'

'Boiled worms and slug juice,' Melissa said crossly. She'd gone out of her way to cook him a decent meal, and he was acting as if he'd found her going through his wallet.

'I don't expect you to cook for me,' he said. 'I told you I'd have managed just fine with cereal.'

'It's not a big deal,' she muttered. Evidently the genius who'd said that the route to man's heart was through his stomach hadn't met Samir Razdan. He sounded positively put out—

as if she'd transgressed some unwritten rule by cooking him a meal.

'Thanks anyway,' he said.

She poured the pasta sauce she'd made earlier over the spaghetti and he took the plate from her. Melissa watched as he took a bite.

'Hey, this is good,' he said, sounding surprised. 'Much better than the stuff Kamala turns out.'

'My dad runs a restaurant, remember?'

'Yes of course—I'd forgotten. So you're quite the little Tarla Dalal, aren't you?'

It was said in an indulgent way, but Melissa decided he was being unnecessarily patronising.

'Not really,' she said, turning away to clear up the kitchen counter. 'If I was Tarla the spaghetti would have been pure vegetarian, and you'd not have eaten more than two bites. Tell me if you want some more, otherwise I'll put this lot in the fridge and go to bed.'

He could move as silently as a panther when he wanted to—Melissa gasped as she felt his hands come up to span her waist.

'Aren't you coming to bed with me?' he murmured, nibbling gently at the nape of her neck.

He knew exactly where the sensitive spot was, and she squirmed helplessly in his arms, finally managing to gasp out, 'Go and finish your dinner.'

'I will…I will.' He turned her around to face him, dipping his head to drop a light kiss on her lips. 'Why so stroppy today?'

Melissa raised her eyebrows. 'You clearly have different standards for yourself and for other people,' she said. 'If I'm stroppy, you're the Grinch. Samir, stop it!'

His mouth came down on hers, warm and sexy and tasting of tangy spaghetti sauce. Melissa resisted half-heartedly for a few seconds, then gave in and let him have his way. Grinch or not, he kissed like a dream—no point wasting a kiss just because she was a little upset with him.

'Still stroppy?' he asked when he finally raised his head.

Melissa shook her head. 'No, just very thankful I didn't put garlic in the pasta.'

He laughed at that, his amazing mouth curving up at the corners. 'You're really something,' he said, and there wasn't the slightest hint of anything patronising in his voice.

'I am,' she agreed solemnly. She was over her temporary fit of annoyance. 'Actually, I'm almost perfect. I write well, I'm very intelligent, I can cook, I'm quite pretty…'

'And incredibly modest as well,' Samir agreed as he moved away to pick up his plate.

'Yes, that too,' she said. 'Hurry up and finish eating now. I want to go to bed.'

He gave her a slow, heart-stopping smile, and she blushed furiously but stood her ground.

'Hmm…' he said. 'I'll be done in a minute—just taking another helping. I'm hungrier than I thought I was.'

She waited while he emptied the rest of the pasta onto his plate, then took the pan from him and rinsed it under the tap. Something had just struck her, and it made a lot of small, rather puzzling incidents fall into place.

'You don't like the thought of me settling in here too thoroughly, do you?' she asked, and his eyes flew up to meet hers immediately, a wary look in them.

'I don't know what you mean,' he said.

Melissa gave him a long, assessing look. 'Oh, I think you do,' she said cheerfully. 'You asked me to move in with you on impulse, because we were both pretty much dying of frustration, and now you're not sure you did the right thing. And every time I do something, like rearrange your CDs or cook you dinner, you start getting worried.'

Samir looked incredulous. 'What would I be worried about?'

'Now that I'm not too sure of,' Melissa admitted, giving him a sunny smile. 'Like I said, I'm very intelligent, but in this case I don't have enough data to go on. Maybe you're worried that I'll become a fixture here and when you're sick of me you won't be able to turf me out. Or that you'll get so used to having me around that you'll be heartbroken when I decide to leave. Or that Kamala will stop working for you because I've taken over the kitchen.'

'Or that little green aliens will come down and take over the planet,' Samir said, laughing. 'You have a really active imagination, Melissa.'

'And now you're acting all superior and patronising because you know I'm right,' Melissa said firmly.

'Melissa…'

'You might as well admit that I'm right.'

'You're not,' Samir said, exasperated. 'Stop being childish. I might be a little stand-offish at times, but there's a lot going on in my life. It doesn't have anything to do with you.'

'Does too.'

Goaded beyond endurance, Samir reached out and grabbed Melissa by her shoulders. She went utterly still as soon as he touched her, her eyes seeming to grow larger as she looked up at him. Torn between wanting to shake her and kiss her senseless, he ended up attempting the latter. She made a strangled little sound as his mouth fastened on hers but she was anything but reluctant, going by the way her arms went around him and her body moulded itself to his.

'You're a big bully,' she said breathlessly when he finally let her go. 'And you know I'm right.'

'A bully, am I?' he asked, looking pointedly at her arms, which were still twined lovingly around him.

'Yes,' she confirmed, leaning up to press a little kiss onto his mouth. 'A gorgeous one, but a bully all the same. No, *don't* do that again.' Determinedly, she wriggled out of his grip. 'I'm not going to be kissed into agreeing with you. Come on, Samir, be serious for a minute.'

He laughed, charmed back into good humour by the kiss and by her uniquely pragmatic way of looking at things.

'Think about it,' she urged. 'Aren't you a little uncomfortable with having let me into your life so easily?'

Samir leaned back a little, exhaling slowly. Melissa was right. He'd wanted her to move in, and he wanted her to stay, but there was still a part of him that was deeply uneasy about sharing his life with another human being.

'Only because I've had a bad experience in the past,' he said finally. 'It's not about you. I wouldn't have asked you to come and live with me if I didn't want you to be part of my life. What's funny?'

It had gone as quickly as it had come, but he knew he hadn't been mistaken about the flash of amusement he'd seen in her eyes.

'Sorry,' she said quickly. 'I told you in Goa— you look like the hero of a romance novel. And now you tell me you have a tortured past. And then you say things like "It's not about you". You're just too in character to be true.'

'Glad to be so entertaining,' he said, trying to keep the wryness out of his tone. 'I'm sure the way you regularly cut me down to size is good for my soul.'

'I'm sorry,' she said, suddenly contrite. 'I don't know what happened to you, and I've no right to make fun of it. God knows I've got a messed up past myself.'

He pushed a hand through his hair, the gesture so unconsciously sexy that Melissa's breath caught in her throat. It would be very easy to fall in love with Samir—she'd spent the past few weeks consciously guarding against it. Telling herself repeatedly that this was a short-lived thing had helped. So had determinedly seeing the funny side of things that could otherwise be upsetting or hurtful.

'It wasn't anywhere as exciting as what happened to you,' Samir said. 'In retrospect, I'm rather embarrassed about it—but I was very young then. I fell madly in love with a woman everyone except me knew was interested in me only because of my money.'

Some of her puzzlement must have shown in her face because he said, 'I inherited a fair bit from my grandparents. And I had a bright career ahead of me.'

'How did you find out?'

He smiled briefly. 'I was going through a

self-discovery phase pretty soon after we got engaged. I thought I'd switch careers, do something I enjoyed. Trouble was, the stuff I enjoyed wasn't high-paying. And I wanted to use most of the money I'd inherited to go and live in Europe for a few years—she was out of the door the minute she realised I was actually serious.'

'What was it that you wanted to do?' Melissa asked curiously. So far he hadn't given the impression of being particularly passionate about anything—definitely not to the extent of giving up his expensive lifestyle. He worked very hard, but it didn't look as if he enjoyed that much either—it was difficult to think of him wanting to go off and follow a dream at any age.

'Ah, that's another story,' he said, taking her hand and switching off the kitchen light as he led her out of the door. 'Anyway, as it turned out I changed my mind and took up a corporate career instead.'

'So if your girlfriend had stuck with you she'd have got all your lovely money after all,' Melissa said. 'Sounds like there's a moral in there somewhere.'

'She married a richer guy,' he said. 'So all in all I think it worked out well for her. And, Melissa…?'

They were inside the bedroom now, and she turned towards him at the suddenly serious note in his voice.

He touched her face gently—a fleeting caress that somehow had more feeling in it than all that they had shared earlier. 'If I've been shutting you out at times, it's because I've got used to being alone. Not because I don't trust you, or because I think you're like Shalini in any way.'

Melissa nodded. 'And, for the record, I'm not trying to push you into anything either. I know you're not in the market for a serious relationship right now and neither am I. Whenever we decide to call it quits we'll be able to do it without a fuss.'

The conversation had become a lot more serious than she'd intended it to. Served her right for nagging at him just because he hadn't been enthusiastic about his home-cooked spaghetti dinner. The next time he worked late she'd just hand him a takeaway menu.

Trying to lighten things up a bit, she added, 'But while I'm living here you'll have to get used to me invading every part of the house. Kitchen and CD rack included.'

Samir turned and caught her into his arms. 'You can invade what you damn well please,' he said, the words warm against her mouth. 'Just as long as you come back to my bed every night.'

CHAPTER SIX

'DON'T FORGET ABOUT the dinner tonight,' Samir warned Melissa as she got out of the car in front of the agency. 'I've got meetings at Maximus the whole day—I'll send the car for you and meet you directly at the party.'

The last time they'd planned to go out for dinner Samir had come home to find Melissa sitting at her laptop in a tattered pair of pyjamas, happily humming under her breath as she worked on her latest writing project. The minor fact that they had a reservation at one of the most exclusive restaurants in town had completely slipped her mind.

This time, though, it was hardly likely she'd forget the party, Melissa thought as Samir drove off. It was a kind of milestone in their relationship, because it was the first time she'd be meeting any of Samir's family—the dinner was at his cousin's home to celebrate her fifteenth wedding anniversary.

'Nervous?' Neera asked later as Melissa grabbed the bag with her evening clothes and headed off to the women's room to change.

Melissa grimaced. 'A bit,' she said. 'Samir's cousin is a total socialite. Not quite gossip column material, but she does a lot of fundraisers with NGOs and charities. I've never met that kind of person before—I'm dreading it.'

'You'll be fine,' Neera said comfortably. 'Just be confident and be yourself. What are you wearing?'

It was easy, telling her to be herself, Melissa thought resentfully. Neera wasn't the one who'd have to go meet a bunch of notoriously bitchy South Mumbai socialites, most of whom would look down their pedigree noses at her. And, while Samir hadn't mentioned it, she knew that more than one woman had nursed hopes of hooking up with him—a lot of those pedigree noses had been put out of joint when she'd appeared on the scene.

SHOMA NARAYANAN 153

She pulled the dress she was planning to wear out of the bag and showed it to Neera. 'Does it look OK?' she asked. It was beige with a black trim and a deceptively simple cut that flattered Melissa's slim figure, making her look taller and curvier at the same time.

Neera wrinkled up her nose. 'It's nice enough, but it's a little dull. Why aren't you wearing the orange dress you bought when we went shopping together to Bandra? That looks great on you—really makes you stand out.'

'I don't want to stand out tonight. I want to blend in,' Melissa retorted. There were several reasons why she'd chosen the beige over the orange—it looked classier, for one, and though it was cheaper it was a far better brand. Export surplus that sold at one fourth of the retail price—but hopefully no one at the party would know that.

When she came out of the cubicle a few minutes later, Neera nodded in approval. 'It looks a lot better with you in it,' she said. 'I wish I had a bust like yours. And a waistline like yours, for that matter. Come here and let me help you with your make-up.'

Ten minutes later she was ready to go, and she slipped her feet into nude pumps as she waved to Neera and hurried out of the office and into the waiting car. 'Mrs Kaul's place in Malabar Hill,' she told Samir's driver.

'Do we pick *sahib* up on the way?' the driver wanted to know.

Melissa shook her head. 'No, he's probably already there. He's hitching a ride with a friend.'

Except that he wasn't—when she reached Priyanka Kaul's plush flat she was told that Samir hadn't yet arrived.

'He messaged me to say that he's running a little late,' Priyanka said in her perfectly modulated voice. 'But it's so lovely to see you. Let me introduce you around to a few people so that you don't get bored. Everyone knows Samir, and they're dying to meet you.'

As far as Melissa was concerned, she could think of nothing worse, but there was no way she could wriggle out of the introductions without being impossibly rude to her hostess.

'So you've actually moved in with Samir?' one of the women asked. She was skinny to the point of emaciation, and had evidently been smoking continuously for a while as the ashtray in front of her was loaded with cigarette butts. 'That's pretty unusual, isn't it? Even in this day and age.'

'Oh, it's very common for advertising agency folk,' another woman said. 'I did a few weeks in an ad agency once when I was really bored. Pretty promiscuous, I thought. Half the women were living with someone or the other. Though I must say most of them had grotty little flats in God-forsaken places like Chandivali and Vasai. Samir's place must be heaven in comparison.'

'Where did you live before you hooked up with Samir?' the first woman asked.

'Colaba,' Melissa said shortly. She didn't explain about the working women's hostel.

Colaba was as nice as you could get in South Mumbai, and the woman looked a little disappointed. She'd probably hoped to hear that Melissa had lived in cockroach-ridden paying guest accommodation miles out of town.

Priyanka came up in time to hear the last bit of the conversation. 'I was so excited when I heard about you,' she said. 'One of my closest friends stays in the same apartment block as Samir, and she told me first. Then, of course, when Samir called next he told me he had a new girlfriend.'

'And a very pretty girlfriend too,' Priyanka's husband said, coming to stand next to her.

'Thanks, Anil,' Melissa muttered, feeling stunned. She'd always thought of Mumbai as being large and anonymous—it had never occurred to her that people she didn't even know might be talking about her and Samir. No wonder Samir was more conscious of appearances than she was.

'Samir's mother will be on the phone with Priyanka as soon as the party's over,' Anil said. 'We're actually more her generation than yours, and she keeps checking in with us about how he's doing. Samir's not the most communicative of sons.'

His mother? Melissa hadn't realised that Samir's mum even knew she existed, let alone that she was keeping track of the parties she attended and calling up people to ask about her afterwards. Priyanka was frowning at Anil now—evidently he wasn't supposed to have shared that last titbit.

'I wonder what's keeping Samir?' she asked, glancing at her watch. 'He said he'd be here by eight-thirty.'

'It's Janmashtami,' Melissa said. 'There are *dahi-handis* set up all across town and the traffic's bad. He must have got stuck at Worli after he got off the sea link.'

'There's always something or the other happening in this city,' one of Anil's friends said. 'It's terrible the way they hold up everything just because of some archaic festival. It's barbaric, the way they make human pyramids to knock down that ridiculous pot of curds. And all for some piddly cash prize.'

'Ah, but the prize isn't piddly by common man standards,' a third man said.

He was thin and wiry, and his wire-framed spectacles gave him a permanently cynical expression. Vikas Kulkarni—that was his name, Melissa remembered. He was the only person in the group other than Priyanka and Anil that Samir had ever mentioned to her. Evidently a bit of a non-conformist, he gave the rest of the group a slow smile that Anil at least appeared to find intensely annoying. 'And, as for being barbaric, wasn't it one of *you* who was raving about breaking *piñatas* in Mexico?'

The man who'd originally called the festival barbaric flushed and was about to say something when Priyanka broke in, 'Oh, but it's not the same thing at all—is it, Vikas? I can't imagine why people would want to spend months practising for something like the *dahi-handi*.'

'It's rather fun, actually,' Melissa said. 'Last year a group of us joined an all-girls team and we used to practise three days a week.'

She didn't add that practising had been far

more fun that the actual Janmashtami celebrations—the *pandals* had been packed with people and one of the girls had been groped in the
crowd. Oh, and they hadn't won anything because the team had been able to form only five
tiers of the pyramid. Other girl *govinda* teams
were able to do six, and male teams went up to
seven and eight.

There was a second's silence—they all looked
as shocked as if she'd confessed to soliciting
customers at Kamathipura on weekends, Melissa thought, trying to stifle the fit of giggles
that threatened to overcome her. Even Vikas,
the spectacled non-conformist, looked a little
taken aback.

'Did you win?' Priyanka's thirteen-year-old
daughter asked interestedly.

Damn kids—they always came up with questions one didn't want to answer.

Melissa shook her head. 'We weren't good
enough,' she said succinctly.

'It's about participating, Nysa, not winning,'
Priyanka said in reproving tones.

Vikas winked at Nysa. 'Remind her she said that when you appear for your board exams,' he said, and everyone laughed.

Priyanka grimaced. 'One can tell you don't have kids, Vikas,' she said. 'You're such a subversive influence.'

Nysa sidled up to Melissa. 'Mum says you write ads?' she asked. 'And you won an award at the festival?'

Melissa nodded. Priyanka and Samir didn't look like each other at all, but there was a strong resemblance between Nysa and him—a throwback to a previous generation, perhaps.

'I read some of your ads,' Nysa said. 'They're, like, quite cool. Though I didn't like the baby one that much—the one that got the award.'

Melissa smiled. There was something rather endearing about the girl.

'Samir Uncle says that's because I'm not part of the target audience,' Nysa went on. 'Sounds weird. Target audience. Like you're at rifle class or something. That's my target audience—boom-boom.'

OK, this was surreal. Samir had discussed her ads with his cousin's daughter. What was she, a specialist subject for their next family quiz show? Trying not to show her annoyance, she smiled dutifully at Nysa's joke.

'D'you want to see around the house?' Nysa asked. 'You haven't been here before, have you?'

'Yes, sure,' Melissa said. It would be better than standing around trying to be polite to a bunch of people she devoutly hoped she'd never have to meet again in her life.

The house was large and furnished with the most impeccable taste—it still felt like a home, though, and not like a museum, and Melissa felt some of her initial hostility fade. People's spaces said a lot about them. Samir's flat screamed 'keep your distance', but this one invited you in, made you feel welcome.

'And this is my room,' Nysa said, throwing open a dark blue door at the end of a passage-way.

As expensively furnished as the other rooms, it was still a typical teenager's cluttered mess, with boy band posters on the walls and clothes strewn extravagantly over every possible surface. What caught Melissa's attention, though, was a big drum set that occupied half the room.

'This is yours?' she asked, and immediately wished she hadn't. Who else's would it be—Priyanka's? No wonder teenagers thought that adults were as thick-headed as turnips.

'Yes,' Nysa said and added gloomily, 'Mum got the door soundproofed. She wanted me to learn the violin.'

Melissa couldn't help grinning at that—though she didn't blame Priyanka, really. With her waif-like build and waist-length hair Nysa would look perfect in a white floaty dress on a concert stage.

She stepped into the room and shut the soundproof door behind her. 'May I?' she asked, gesturing towards the drumsticks that Nysa was fiddling with.

Nysa's 'You *play*?' was almost as incredulous as Priyanka's reaction to her *govinda* skills.

'You bet I do,' Melissa said, pulling up a

stool and grabbing the sticks before Nysa could change her mind. 'My brother taught me—I took his place in the college band when he graduated.'

My God, it felt brilliant, getting her hands on the drums again. Even better than being back in a proper kitchen and almost as good as sex. And it was amazing the way the old beats came back to her, though it had been four years since she'd last played on stage.

When Samir arrived ten minutes later Melissa was still holed up with Nysa. 'Happy anniversary,' he said, leaning down to hug his cousin. 'And congratulations on the new project—I believe everyone's completely blown away by it.'

Priyanka had just put together a massive fundraiser for the launch of a new medical charity, and it had been a spectacular success.

Samir's eyes automatically scanned the room for a familiar slim figure. 'Priyanka, where's Melissa?' he asked. He hadn't checked if she'd reached the party OK—for a second all kinds of horrifying scenarios crossed his mind.

Priyanka looked up from the designer arrangement of silk flowers he'd given her. 'Oh, she's around,' she said. 'I think Nysa took her to show her round the house. Such a sweet girl.'

'Who? Nysa?' Samir asked, grinning because he knew who she meant.

Priyanka shuddered. 'Nysa's a nightmare right now,' she said. 'Going through one of those teenage phases. I meant Melissa—she's so sparky and confident—I'm completely in love with her.'

'And she is going to tell your mother she approves, I believe,' Vikas murmured as he came up to Samir. 'I think you should prepare for some serious pressure from the female half of your family.'

Samir groaned. His mother had graduated from wanting to choose a bride for him to eagerly gathering information about every woman he dated in the hope that he'd finally settle down and give her the grandchildren she wanted.

'I approve too, by the way,' Vikas said.

Samir frowned. Vikas was notoriously picky

and difficult to please. 'What exactly has Melissa been doing since she got here?'

Vikas put his head to one side, rather like an inquisitive sparrow. 'Wellll,' he drawled, ticking off the points on his fingers, 'she's managed to deal with your bitchy ex-admirers over there without bursting into tears or clawing their eyes out. And she put a bunch of people in their place when they sneered at *dahi-handis*. She's corrected my English twice—once when I said "keep" instead of "put" and once when I said "improvise" when I meant "improve". And now she's gone off to play drums with Priyanka's daughter, I believe. I went inside to use the washroom and the door to that kid's room isn't as soundproof as our hosts would like to believe. Nysa's not bad at the drums, but she's still learning. I'll eat my best tie if it's her playing right now.'

Luckily Vikas didn't have to perform the threatened gastronomic feat, because when Samir pushed open the door to Nysa's room Melissa was banging out a hard rock rhythm while Nysa gazed at her in awestruck admiration. Her cheeks were glowing with the effort, and her flyaway hair had come loose and was tumbling around her shoulders.

'Oh, you're here,' she said, pausing mid-beat and looking up at him, evidently conscience-stricken at having abandoned the party. 'I'm so sorry. I lost track of the time a little.'

Samir had a sudden impulse to sweep her off her feet and kiss her—she looked so naturally lovely. But Vikas and Nysa were looking on interestedly, so he contented himself with dropping a chaste kiss on her brow and putting an arm around her as he shepherded her to the door.

Melissa found the rest of the evening surprisingly enjoyable. Vikas was clearly a bit of a trendsetter among Priyanka's friends, and because he'd taken an abrupt liking to Melissa the others started treating her less like an interloper. Samir didn't speak much, but she was conscious of his quiet strength by her side all along.

'Wasn't as terrible as you thought it would be, right?' Samir asked later as they drove home.

Melissa shot him a startled look, and he laughed.

'You're pretty easy to read,' he said, putting a hand on her knee and sending an automatic little thrill up her thigh. 'Relax—they all loved you.'

Really? she felt like saying. *What about the two women I met at the beginning?* They'd still looked at her as if she was some kind of cheap slut when she left.

'As far as I'm concerned it's more important what I thought of them than what they thought of me,' she announced. 'I liked Vikas, and your cousin and Nysa. Didn't really care for the rest.'

That was so typical, Samir thought, half amused and half exasperated. He was conscious that he'd wanted to see if she'd fit into his circle—it was important that she did if they were to have any kind of future together. She'd done amazingly well, keeping up a light, easy conversation without being sycophantic or intimidated. Trust her to have a completely different take on the situation, though.

When they got home Melissa brushed her teeth and went to bed while Samir was checking the mail that had come for him during the day. It had been a long day, and she was a little upset, and frankly feeling rather stupid. Of *course* he was more worried about her making some dreadful faux pas in front of his friends than he was about whether she liked them or not. She'd been dumb to think that her opinion would matter to him in the slightest.

Feeling hot tears prick at her eyelids, she blinked them back. It wasn't the end of the world, being at cross purposes with a boyfriend. She should be used to it by now—it had happened before. But Josh hadn't given out confusing signals like Samir did—he'd just not been in love with her.

Samir hadn't said he was in love with her either, but it was clear he was serious about their relationship. Introducing her to his cousin and his friends had made it seem as if he wanted to take things to the next level—as far as Melissa was concerned, though, she'd be happier if they first made up their minds about each other before they got other people involved.

Only Samir hadn't asked her. He'd evidently expected that she'd be overjoyed at the thought of being his official girlfriend rather than staying tucked away in an airtight corner of his life.

Wondering if she was being madly unreasonable, Melissa squeezed her eyes tightly closed and rubbed at her forehead with her knuckles. No, she decided, opening her eyes again. He needed to talk things over with her before he went off making one-sided decisions and subjecting her to being assessed by his family.

Samir came into the bedroom, and she turned towards the wall and pretended to be asleep.

CHAPTER SEVEN

THE NEXT DAY was a Sunday, and Melissa woke up at six-thirty to the sound of bells ringing in a nearby church.

She lay in bed and listened to the chimes die away. It had been over a year since she'd last gone to church, she realised. When she'd first come to Mumbai she'd gone with Liz to a church in Colaba almost every Sunday. Then slowly inertia had crept in and she'd started going less often, then stopped altogether.

There was a large church near Samir's apartment complex—maybe she'd try going there one Sunday. Samir was Hindu, of course, and from what she could make out not particularly religious. But he'd studied in a Catholic school for some years, and in the course of a general conversation she'd figured out that he knew more about Catholic customs than Hindu ones.

Maybe he'd want to come with her to church. Or maybe not.

She turned to look at Samir. He was still fast asleep, one hand possessively clasping her hip and the other pillowing his cheek. His breathing was even and his face was smooth and untroubled. Clearly he'd gone to sleep the second his head hit the pillow instead of staying up half the night obsessing about a relationship that was going nowhere.

He sighed and shifted a little closer, automatically seeking the warmth of her body. It would be so *easy* to stop bothering about the complicated stuff and just let things happen.

Slowly, she slid out from under Samir's arm, putting it on a pillow instead. He didn't seem to mind in the least, and she smiled grimly. She was probably equally replaceable when he was awake, only he hadn't realised it yet.

After she'd brushed her teeth and washed her face she felt much better. Best of all she'd regained some of her sense of humour—enough to be able to laugh at herself and her silly problems. It wasn't the end of the world, liking some-one more than they liked you—high school was full of such tragedies. Or at least it was for other people. Melissa herself had had a pretty good time in school. It was when she was all grown up that her man problems had begun.

Humming to herself, she went into the kitchen and started investigating the shelves. She'd found a wonderful little store that delivered pro-visions, and the kitchen was now beautifully stocked. As usual, just being in the kitchen made her mood lift up several notches. Now all she needed was a nice calorie-rich break-fast to get her back to being a hundred percent normal.

'Something smells nice,' Samir said, putting his head around the kitchen door after ten min-utes. 'What're you making?'

'Pancakes,' she said and added wickedly, be-cause she knew how particular he was about eating healthily, 'loaded with sugar and butter and refined carbs.'

'Oh, well, I'll just have to spend an extra half-hour in the gym,' he said. 'Or you could help me burn those calories in a more fun way...'

Melissa skipped neatly out of the way as he reached for her. 'Keep your hands to yourself,' she said, rapping him on the knuckles with a wooden spatula. 'I'm busy.'

The doorbell rang just as he was about to grab her around the waist, and he paused. 'Will you go and answer the door?' he asked.

'Absolutely not,' Melissa said. 'I'm not wearing a bra.'

Samir thought it over. 'Neither am I,' he said. 'So as excuses go...'

He dodged the dishcloth that Melissa threw at his head and went off laughing to open the door.

Five minutes later he was back. 'It's my financial consultant,' he said, making a wry face. 'I completely forgot I'd made an appointment to go over my portfolio. I'll try and finish as fast as I can.'

'Take your time,' Melissa said, waving a spatula at him. 'And ask your financial consultant if he'd like some pancakes.'

'It's a she,' Samir said, giving her the quirky smile he reserved for when he was pulling her leg. 'I'm surprised at you, Melissa, making gender-based assumptions like that. She won't have pancakes—I don't think she's eaten any carbs for the last decade or so. Save my share for me, OK?'

Once the pancakes were done, Melissa wandered into the TV room with her plate and put the TV on. As usual it took her a little while to figure out the various remotes for the satellite dish, the TV and the home theatre system, and when she finally did get the TV on and tried switching channels it insisted on playing one regional language channel after another. Another minute's tussle got her onto the satellite TV menu, and with a sigh of relief she chose a popular Hindi movie channel.

It was playing an old movie, set in Kashmir, with the obligatory *shikaras* on a lake being rowed by pink-cheeked damsels in traditional Kashmiri costumes. A sucker for old-fashioned romances, Melissa settled down with her stack of pancakes to watch the lead pair coo lovingly at each other. *Ooh*, they were so *sweet*, in their horrendous clothes and bright make-up. It had been a while since she'd watched an old movie—there was only one TV in the hostel, and people preferred chick-flicks and action movies to vintage Bollywood.

She was completely engrossed in the movie when the channel was changed abruptly. Melissa swung around to see Samir holding the remote.

'Hey, I was watching that!' she said indignantly as she grabbed at the remote.

Samir held it away from her, easily fending her off with one hand.

'It's an awful movie,' he said. 'Really, really terrible.'

It probably was, but that wasn't the point—he hadn't even bothered to ask her before changing channels. Granted, it was his home, but that didn't give him the right to be high-handed about every damn thing.

'I like it,' Melissa said, and when he didn't

give her the remote she got up and went to the
TV to change the channel manually.

'Melissa…' he said, and the slightly strained
note in his voice made her stop in her tracks.
'Look, I *really* don't want to watch that movie.'

'O-kay,' she said slowly. 'Is there a particular reason, or are you just Bollywood-phobic?'

He hesitated, and then shook his head as if to
clear it of cobwebs. 'Something like that,' he
said. 'But if you want to watch it don't let me
stop you. I can always go somewhere else and
read a magazine.'

Hmm…fifty-year-old movie or thirty-year-old
boyfriend? Not much of a choice, really—especially not when Samir was looking so incredibly hot. His hair was still damp from the
shower, and it was falling over his forehead in
sexy spikes, and he smelt amazing.

Wishing she'd had just a little more practice
at being seductive and alluring, she said, 'Or
we could do something together.'

He raised an eyebrow. 'Play chess?'

'I was thinking Scrabble,' she said solemnly,

and he laughed, coming up to her and running the backs of his fingers down the side of her face very, very slowly.

She shivered with anticipation as his hand slipped lower, to the neckline of her dress, and she gasped aloud as he finally gave up toying with her and pulled her ruthlessly into his arms.

It was much later, when they were having lunch, that Melissa asked, 'Why didn't you want to watch that movie? It was like you couldn't bear to look at the screen.'

He was silent for almost a minute, and Melissa began to wish she'd stayed off the topic. Then he said slowly, 'It was the location. The movie was shot in the town I used to live in as a kid. We had to leave the valley after militants razed the area—we were one of the few families lucky enough to escape alive.'

Melissa stared at him. 'I didn't know,' she said awkwardly. She'd been reading about the insurgency in the valley for years—the newspapers

were full of it—but this was the first time she'd
met anyone who'd been personally affected.

Samir shrugged. 'No big deal,' he said. 'Like
I said, we were lucky to get out of there alive.
Lots of people we knew didn't make it.'

There wasn't much she could say to that, and
she stayed silent. It was ironic, she thought.
There she'd been, obsessing about how little
Samir knew and understood her, and it turned
out she knew even less about him. If someone
had asked her which state he was from she'd
probably would have said Punjab—she didn't
know enough about Hindu surnames to be able
to place people by state. She'd not really thought
about it much, other than once idly remarking
that his colouring was typically North Indian—
fair skin with dark but not quite black eyes and
hair.

'I didn't have you pegged as a Hindi movie
buff,' Samir said when the silence had stretched
on long enough to be unnatural.

'I'm not,' Melissa said, shaking her head vig-
orously. 'I just like soppy movies. I'd watch

them even if they were in Swahili. I'm thinking of writing a book about them one day.'

'Seriously?'

'Well, I might. There's a guy who's written one about Hindi blockbusters—it's pretty good. But there's something else I'm working on right now. If I ever find a publisher for that, I'll start working on this one.'

'What's the first one? A cookbook?' he asked.

He hadn't meant to sound patronising, but she seemed to gravitate to the kitchen whenever she was free and it was a natural assumption. It was only when her expression changed that he realised that he'd upset her.

'Not really,' she said. 'Anyway, it's at a very basic stage—I've a long way to go.'

Samir hesitated a little. He'd picked up on the way Melissa reacted to some of the things he said, only he didn't know which particular statement would set her off. Yesterday it had been what he'd said about his friends liking her, today it was her book… If it had been any other woman he'd have written her off as being over-sensitive and too high-maintenance to bother with. But Melissa didn't really say anything or create a scene. It was just by the way her lovely mouth turned down at the corners and a crease appeared between her eyebrows that he knew she was upset, and he'd begun watching her face like a hawk for the tell-tale signs.

Right now she seemed to be over her annoyance, so he let the subject slide. 'What do you want to do in the afternoon?' he asked.

Melissa jumped to her feet. 'Let's go to the art gallery near Flora Fountain,' she said. 'There's a new artist holding an exhibition there who's supposed to be really good.'

Samir grimaced. He didn't mind buying the occasional piece, recommended by a more knowledgeable friend, but given a choice he'd rather spend the afternoon getting a root canal done than wandering around an art gallery.

He didn't protest, though, and even feigned some enthusiasm as he followed Melissa out of the door. Another first for him, he thought. After Shalini he'd never bothered putting what a woman wanted to do ahead of what he wanted himself. And it would have been staggeringly easy to distract Melissa. For all her feistiness, a few kisses were usually enough to turn her into putty in his hands.

'I can see that your girlfriend is quite the dominatrix,' Vikas Kulkarni murmured when they bumped into him at the gallery. 'And you might want to watch out for that artist dude. He seems quite taken with her.'

Vikas was right, Samir realised as he looked across the room. The artist was ignoring a well-heeled couple who were on the point of buying one of his paintings in order to earnestly explain something to Melissa. Muttering an oath under his breath, he strode across to the two of them. Putting up with Melissa's whims was one thing. Allowing her to be chatted up by a skinny, long-haired artist was quite another.

The man looked up in alarm as Samir came up to them. 'I was just telling Melissa the thought behind this painting,' he mumbled defensively.

Samir surveyed the painting. From what he

could see it was a set of random splodges of paint. Presumably it had some deep meaning, but as far as he was concerned it was a waste of a perfectly good piece of canvas. Melissa seemed entranced by it, though, because she kept on standing in front of it even when the artist went off to attend to the couple who were now getting decidedly impatient.

'If you really like it I'll buy it for you,' Samir said finally.

Her eyes widened. 'But it costs over a hundred thousand!' she exclaimed after looking at the price tag. 'The guy must be smoking something—pricing it so high.'

'It's a brilliant investment,' Vikas said, strolling up to them. 'Shekhar will be big in a couple of years. You've got a good eye for art, kiddo. This is the best piece in the show.'

'Let's buy it, then,' Samir said, trying not to show his annoyance at the interruption, and impressed in spite of himself. If Vikas said the piece was good, it definitely was, and he couldn't help feeling proud of the way Melissa had homed in on it.

Melissa looked tempted for a few seconds, but then she shook her head firmly. 'I've no place to hang it,' she said. 'It's huge. I could put it up in your place for as long as I'm there, but afterwards I'd have to stick legs on it and use it as a cot.'

Vikas gave a suppressed snort of laughter and Samir finally lost his temper. 'Let's go, then,' he said crisply. 'I don't see the point of hanging around and wasting everyone's time if we're not planning to buy anything.'

Melissa waited till they were back in the car park opposite the gallery before she said tentatively, 'Are you upset?'

Samir glared at her. 'I'm not upset,' he said. 'I'm flaming furious. What possessed you to start babbling about putting legs on a canvas in front of that old gossip Vikas? You made me look like an absolute fool.'

She was staring at him, her eyes wide. 'All

I meant was that whenever we split up I won't have any place to put that painting!'

'*When* we split up. It's not even *if* for you, is it? God knows I've done enough to try and make it work—asking you to move in with me, introducing you to my friends, letting you have your way with all your little whims and fancies. But *nothing* convinces you to try and give us a fighting chance!'

'I didn't know you *wanted* us to have a fighting chance!' she protested, her eyes turning bright with unshed tears. 'Stop shouting at me, Samir. I don't even know what I've done wrong.'

Samir shut his eyes for a second and rubbed at his forehead. 'All right, let's start from the beginning,' he said. 'I'm sorry I yelled at you. All I'm trying to say is that it's hurtful when you just assume that we don't have a future together.'

Hurtful? Melissa turned that thought over in her mind carefully, too surprised to stay upset. She hadn't imagined that anything she said or did would have the power to hurt Samir. Apparently, she'd been wrong.

'I thought it was…safer,' she said after a bit. 'We started off thinking it would be a holiday fling kind of thing, and then it got more serious. I wanted to make sure I didn't read more into it than you wanted me to.'

Samir took her hand. 'That was partly my fault,' he admitted. 'But I've never met anyone like you before. I've been trying to figure things out as we go along.'

'That makes two of us,' Melissa said, giving him a watery smile. 'Maybe we should just try talking a little more from now on? Just a thought.'

'It might work,' he said, but when she started to reply he stifled the words against her lips. 'Not right now, though,' he whispered, his warm breath mingling with hers. 'I can think of more exciting ways to make up.'

The next Monday morning, when Samir walked into the Mendonca Advertising office, he found

Melissa busily clearing out her desk. For a second an icy hand clutched at his heart. Then he remembered that she was changing jobs. She'd be joining Nexus, Maya Kumar's agency, next Monday—she was taking this week off to relax.

'I'll miss seeing you around,' he murmured as he bent over her on the pretext of helping her put some of her things into a carton.

She blushed and said softly, 'I'll miss you too. But at least I won't get distracted when I'm supposed to be working.'

The thought that he had the ability to distract her was hugely pleasing, he realised, barely able to stop a smile from spreading across his face. The weekend had been pretty amazing, once they'd sorted out their misunderstanding, and he knew Melissa had been quite as blown away by it as he was.

'Are you coming to my farewell lunch?' she asked. 'Devdeep's asked me a dozen times through the morning.'

'I guess so,' he said. 'Where are they holding it?'

'The Parsi café opposite the office,' she said, and added quickly as she saw him frown, 'Don't ask them to change the venue, please. That's where they've always held agency celebrations—it's a bit of a Mendonca tradition. And Brian's coming too.'

The restaurant was run by a pair of elderly, slightly wacky Parsi brothers who'd known Brian for years. In spite of its grungy appearance the kitchen was as hygienic as the average five-star restaurant, and the food was a dozen times better. Though most of Melissa's colleagues seemed more interested in the bottles of ice-cold beer than in the food.

Melissa shook her head as Brian offered her a bottle. 'I don't like the taste,' she said. 'But you go ahead. I'm so thrilled you could make it, Brian!'

'He wouldn't have missed your farewell party for the world, *dikra*,' said Cyrus, the older of the two brothers, as he leaned over her shoulder to plonk a plate of mutton *dhansak* in front of her. 'And if he'd still been running that agency of yours I bet a million rupees you wouldn't have left.'

'Shh,' Melissa said, casting an agonised look at Samir, but he seemed more amused than offended.

Darius, the other brother, chimed in. 'Melissa, forget this whole agency rubbish and come and work with *us*. We'll make this the best restaurant in town.'

'What do you mean by that? It's already the best restaurant in town,' Cyrus huffed, but he gave Melissa an affectionate look. 'Not that you wouldn't be a whiz at running this place, Melly. We're both getting a bit too old to manage it.'

'Speak for yourself,' Darius muttered.

Melissa stood up and hugged both of them in turn—she couldn't help it. 'I'll come here for lunch every Saturday,' she said. 'And the day you give me a stake in the restaurant I'll quit my job and come and join you.'

It was amazing, the way she developed a rapport with all kinds of people, Samir thought, feeling a little glow of pride as he watched

Melissa. He himself found it easy to establish working relationships with most people, but he was close only to his own kind—the people who had been to the right schools, who spoke with the right accent.

Brian leaned across the table. 'I can't believe you're letting her go,' he said. 'That girl's a star.'

Samir looked back at him, his good mood evaporating immediately. 'I have my reasons,' he said evenly. 'And I told you when I took over, Brian: I'm a businessman, not an ad man. I'm here to get the financials into shape before I hand over to someone who knows how to run the place.'

His annoyance with Brian persisted when on the way home Melissa said, 'It was so good to see Brian again.'

'It was hardly a surprise,' he said stiffly. 'I don't suppose he has much to do—he must have been looking forward to this lunch for weeks.'

'You don't like him much, do you?' Melissa said slowly.

Samir shrugged. 'He's all right. To be honest,

I'm a little irritated by the way he kept telling me that I shouldn't have let you leave. He knows perfectly well that there were personal reasons behind the decision. And left to himself he'd have run the agency into the ground—each and every one of you would have been out of a job.'

'But he didn't let that happen, did he?' Melissa said. 'He sold the place to Maximus even though he hated the idea.'

'He made a pot of money in the deal,' Samir snorted. 'Though, knowing how impractical he is, he'll probably give most of it away.'

'We're squabbling again,' Melissa said, suddenly conscience-stricken. 'And I was so sure we wouldn't, after that talk we had.'

Samir laughed. 'It's natural to squabble,' he said. 'The same way it's natural for me to feel a bit jealous of Brian. I know you wouldn't have changed jobs if he was still in charge.'

Completely disarmed by the admission, she leaned across and hugged him, narrowly missing sending the car into a ditch.

'Whoa—careful,' he said, putting an arm around her and giving her a brief hug.

'You're amazing,' she said. 'Have I told you recently how amazing you are?'

Samir grinned. 'Not recently enough,' he said. 'Looking forward to the new job?'

Melissa nodded. 'I am. I won't be working directly with Maya, of course—she's way too senior—but she was so encouraging at the interview that I can't wait to join.'

This time Samir didn't voice it, but he felt a little left out in her enthusiasm for the move. He'd been a bit surprised at her decision to change jobs—especially when the hours at her new place were likely to be so much longer.

'What are you planning to do this week?'

'Work on my book project, mainly,' Melissa said. 'I won't get much time once I start the new job, and Maya said she wanted to take a look at it. I'd like to do another round of edits before I show it to her.'

Samir frowned. 'Is that a good idea?' he asked. 'She's your new employer, and at least at the beginning you should come across as being fully committed to your job. I mean, writing a book isn't the same as writing copy for ads—she might think you're not concentrating on what she's employing you for.'

'I didn't think of it that way,' Melissa said. 'It came up in the interview and she wanted to tell me about an opportunity to do a short story for a magazine.'

Maya Kumar had actually been very encouraging—she'd asked to see samples of Melissa's work, and she'd actually read the stories and given her feedback on them. Melissa found she didn't feel like telling Samir those details, though. Evidently, he didn't think her important enough for someone like Maya to be interested in her work, and anything she said would only come out sounding as if she was trying to blow her own trumpet.

'I still think you should keep the book thing a little low-key for now,' Samir said. 'But it's great that she's interacting with you directly, given how senior she is.'

'Yes, it's brilliant,' Melissa said, unable to keep the sarcasm out of her voice.

Samir looked up immediately. While Melissa was supremely confident about her copywriting abilities, she could get incredibly touchy and secretive about her book. Every time he'd tried discussing it with her he'd found himself inadvertently treading on her toes. He needed training from Maya on how to handle the topic, he thought wryly. She'd evidently hit exactly the right note—Melissa seemed to have elevated her to fairy godmother status.

'I'd like to read your book some time,' he said, trying to backpedal out of the mess he'd got himself into. 'You haven't even told me what it's about.'

'You wouldn't like it,' she said. 'I'm writing it from a completely feminine point of view.'

'I think I can handle it,' he said, but she was already shaking her head.

'Anyway, it's not complete yet. I don't want anyone to see it until I'm happy with what I've done.'

Anyone other than Maya Kumar, evidently, Samir thought, but he didn't say anything. There was no point getting Melissa upset, though he was now feeling very curious about the book. He didn't pretend to be a literary critic, but he knew good writing when he saw it. So far he'd only seen Melissa's advertising work, which was uniformly excellent, but he knew that being a superb copywriter didn't necessarily mean you'd make a good author.

Melissa's book could be brilliant, but it could equally well be trash—and she herself didn't seem confident about it. Hopefully he'd be able to convince her to let him read it soon so that he could form his own opinion.

They were almost home, and there was a brief pause as Samir negotiated a complicated three-point turn to get the car into the apartment complex.

'Dreadful planning,' he muttered as the car shot across the road at right angles to oncoming traffic. 'It's a wonder there hasn't been a car crash here yet.'

'My cabbie always goes straight down the road and takes a turn at the signal,' Melissa said, her lips curving into a smile. 'He says that only careless rich people can afford to take the risk of getting their bumpers dented here.'

Samir, who'd got used to her chatty friendships with everyone she met, grinned. 'So did you tell him that your boyfriend's one of those careless people?'

'Of course not,' Melissa said in her best shocked tones. 'That would have ruined my street cred completely!'

CHAPTER EIGHT

THE LANDLINE WAS ringing when Melissa let herself into the flat, and she dragged her cartons in and dumped them by the door before she went to answer it. Samir had dropped her by the lift and gone to park the car, and Kamala had taken the day off, so there was no one else in the flat.

'Hello?' she said.

There was a brief pause before a woman's voice said, 'Hi. Could I speak to Samir, please?'

'He isn't at home,' Melissa said. There was something vaguely familiar about the voice, but try as she might she couldn't place it. 'Can I take a message?'

'No, that's all right. I'll call him on his cell phone later. Is that Melissa?'

'Um, yes,' Melissa said warily. If this was one

of Samir's ex-girlfriends she really didn't want to get into a conversation with her.

'I'm Bina,' the woman said. 'Do tell Samir I called, OK?'

'I will,' Melissa replied, wondering if she was supposed to know who Bina was.

She'd sounded pretty authoritative, actually— not like an ex, more like an older cousin, or Samir's boss or something. Only, if she was his cousin or his boss wouldn't she have called him on his cell?

Giving up on figuring it out, Melissa went back to the living room to fetch her cartons.

'The more I think about it, the more I realise how much I'll miss you at work,' Samir said when he came in a few minutes later.

'You'll get over it,' Melissa said unsympathetically. 'One of those spreadsheets you keep slogging over will suddenly show that Mendonca's making a profit and you'll be so excited that you'll forget all about me. And, in any case, aren't you going back to Maximus in a couple of months?'

'Well, I'll miss you for those couple of months,' he said. 'And you're completely wrong about the spreadsheets—Mendonca's already showing profits. Devdeep's doing a good job, and it helps that Brian's not around, taking on commissions for peanuts and then giving away most of the money to noble causes.'

Melissa was about to spring to Brian's defence when he took the wind out of her sails.

'Though I must say in all the years I've been working I haven't come across anyone who's as genuinely generous as Brian is.'

Melissa's brows flew up. 'Wow, that's a complete volte-face,' she said. 'Did the lift man slip you a tolerance pill on your way up?'

Samir shrugged. 'He's still a terrible businessman,' he said. 'A guy like Brian would be better off running an NGO.'

Feeling suddenly contrite about the bitchy way she'd reacted, Melissa made an apologetic face. 'Sorry,' she said. 'Volte-face is another one of those swanky phrases I've never used before in real life.'

'At least you'll not get bored with me until you've had a chance to use your entire French vocabulary,' he said lightly.

Melissa ran across the room to him. 'I'll never get bored of you, and I'll miss you at work too,' she said, in a rare burst of candour about her feelings for him. 'I'll be thinking about you all the time.'

Samir swung her off her feet effortlessly and strode towards the bedroom. 'We'll need to make sure we make the best use of the time we have at home,' he said, depositing her carefully on the bed. 'We wouldn't want you getting bored when you think about me.'

It was a while before she remembered the phone call. 'Someone called for you,' she said, pulling away and frowning in an effort to recall the name. 'Bina.'

Samir groaned. 'On the landline?'

'Well, yes. She'd hardly have called you on my cell.'

'You don't know my mother,' Samir said grimly.

Hang on—his *mother*? Melissa stared at him. 'That was your mum? But…she sounded so young! And she didn't *say* she was your mum.'

'She wouldn't.' Samir's smile was wry. 'She's been dying to talk to you ever since she found out about your existence. And anyway she always introduces herself by her first name. She works for a European embassy and she's picked up some of their ways.'

Melissa digested that carefully as Samir swung his feet over the side of the bed and stood up. To her surprise, he didn't reach for his phone immediately. Instead, he opened his wardrobe and pulled out a set of tennis clothes.

'Think I'll go and play tennis for a bit,' he said.

'Why? Didn't you get enough exercise?' Melissa asked waspishly before she could stop herself. Who did he think he was? A world class tennis player?

Samir laughed. 'I did…I did. I just feel like

some fresh air.' He hesitated a little. 'Would you rather that I don't go?'

'Aren't you going to call her back first?' Melissa asked, and when he gave her a blank look, said, 'Your mum?'

He sighed. 'I'll call her. Not right now, though.'

Knowing she should let it go, Melissa couldn't help asking, 'What if she calls again?'

'Tell her that you gave me the message and I said I'd call her back.'

The front door of the flat closed behind him with a firm thud, and Melissa was left staring after him. There had been something definitely odd about the way Samir had reacted, she thought. Come to think of it, he hardly talked about his immediate family—she knew he had a younger brother, and now she knew that his mum worked in an embassy. There had been that one time when he'd told her about their escaping to Delhi when the trouble was at its height in the valley, but other than that he didn't seem to talk about them at all.

On impulse, she picked up her phone and

typed 'Bina Razdan' into a search engine. Her jaw dropped at the number of hits thrown up.

'She works for a European embassy' had been an understatement, implying that she had some kind of clerical job—from what Melissa could see, Samir's mother was a pretty senior diplomat.

It was the first time Melissa had tried to find out more about Samir's family than what he'd voluntarily told her, and she mentally contrasted the picture on the internet of Bina in a silk sari and pearls talking to a powerful politician with her own mother.

Theresa D'Cruz had been a regular mum, wrapped up in her kids and their studies. She'd helped out in her husband's restaurant, and she'd used to sing in the church on weekends. If you'd asked her if she wanted a career, she'd have thought you were pulling her leg.

Trying to imagine what it would be like to have a high-flying diplomat for a mum, Melissa wondered who had picked up Samir from school and helped him with his studies, done the hundred little things mothers were supposed to do.

Then she shook herself. Bina having a career didn't automatically mean that she was a bad mum. In any case, Samir had spent the first ten years of his life in Kashmir—his mum had probably been at home then. And it looked as if his father was a pretty rich businessman—they must have had a luxurious life even after they'd moved to Delhi, because she remembered Samir telling her that his father had moved most of his investments into the capital city when the trouble in the valley escalated.

Slipping off the bed, Melissa went into the bathroom for a quick shower before changing into running shorts and a T-shirt. Time she went and got herself some fresh air as well, she thought. Samir's apartment had a very well-equipped gym attached, but Melissa preferred jogging on the track that ran around the building.

It was almost dark when she hit the track, and it took her a while to settle into a rhythm.

There was hardly anyone in downstairs—Melissa had discovered that most of the neighbours spent their evenings either in front of the TV or eating out at expensive restaurants. One would have expected the place to be eerily silent, but it was actually quite the opposite.

Like most of the new high-end apartments in central Mumbai, Samir's building occupied former mill land. The mills were long gone, but the tenements that had housed the mill workers were still there. Most of the workers were now drivers or cleaners for the rich people who lived in the buildings, and Melissa still found the divide between the rich and the not so rich very unsettling.

It was the first day of the annual Ganpati festival, and the nearest set of tenements had set up a huge marquee where people were in the process of installing a seven-foot-high clay idol of the elephant-headed god. Music blared out from loudspeakers, people were dancing on the roads outside, and a troupe of drummers was enthusiastically giving the dancers their money's worth.

Melissa automatically found her feet hitting the ground in time to the drums. Maybe this could be the next big thing after Tai Chi and Pilates, she thought, grinning to herself—running to the beat of the *dhol.* For a few minutes she was tempted to go out onto the street and watch the Ganpati being hauled into place, but she knew that she'd need to be properly dressed to do that. *Kameez* over jeans at the very least, if not a proper *churidaar kurta* or a sari.

She was still thinking about the Ganpati festival when she rounded a corner and heard a very familiar voice. So Samir hadn't gone to play tennis after all—or if he had he'd ended the game early. He was standing in the car park and speaking into his cell phone. Melissa automatically slowed down, but he was standing with his back towards her and didn't see her.

'*Why* did you call Melissa?' Samir was saying heatedly into the phone. 'Mum, I need you to stay out of this—please. It's very early days, and I haven't made up my mind yet.'

His mother was obviously saying something, and it sounded as if he was cutting her short.

'No, you can't come down to Mumbai right now. Let me figure things out first, OK?'

Figure *what* out? Melissa was standing stock-still now, her face very pale. She could no more have stopped herself from eavesdropping than she could have stopped breathing.

Samir's voice had softened now.

'I'll try and come down to Delhi next week. Yes, I miss you too. I've just been very busy… And it'll be great to see Dad as well.' There was another pause, and then he said, 'God, you're such a *woman*!' But he sounded indulgent now, not annoyed. 'It's difficult to describe her like that. She's very pretty, and she's bright—not the academic type, really, but feisty and street-smart.'

There was yet another pause.

'I don't know if I'm in love with her, Mum.'

Melissa bit her lip. *Of course* he didn't love

her. What had she expected? That he'd confess to having been secretly in love with her since the second he'd clapped his eyes on her?

His mother was evidently still firing questions at him, because he went on.

'I haven't met her family, except for her brother. Seemed a nice enough chap—typical middle-class Goan, runs a restaurant with his dad and plays drums for a local band in his free time. Her mother's dead.'

It wasn't said in a callous way at all, but his last words still cut deep. She hadn't talked about her mother with Samir except the one time he'd asked about her. It wasn't something she spoke about much.

She started walking again, picking up speed as she tried to get away from Samir's line of vision as quickly as possible before he turned around and saw her. *Her mother's dead. Typical middle-class Goan.* Both true, and logically there was no reason for her to be upset. What he *hadn't* said was, *Not our kind of people,* though the implication had come through loud and clear. It matched up with what she'd found out about his family—they were leagues ahead of hers, both in terms of social status as well as wealth and power. Things she'd never ever given importance to because they hadn't directly affected her before.

Her footsteps slowed again once she'd put enough distance between herself and Samir. She felt bewildered and heartsore. Ever since Samir had told her that he was doing his best to make it work between them she'd relaxed her guard and let herself believe that they had a future together. Evidently she'd been fooling herself. Perhaps what had got Samir riled up after their trip to the art gallery was her stubborn insistence that theirs was a short-term affair— presumably the length was something that *he* wanted to dictate.

It was the first time that someone she cared about had made her feel that she was *lacking* in some way. She'd been the youngest in her family—not pampered, exactly, but always valued. Michael and her father had been quietly indulgent during her teenage years, and when Michael had got married, Cheryl had become the older sister Melissa had always wanted. Until, of course, Melissa had ruined everything by taking up with Josh.

For a few seconds Melissa missed home so badly that it was like a physical pain. In spite of the past two years being rocky, she knew that her father and brother loved her deeply. Michael had been calling regularly, and he'd dropped enough hints for her to figure out that her father had been keeping track of her through Liz and Brian ever since she'd left Goa. Maybe that was what she needed to do, she thought—go back and make peace with her 'typical middle-class Goan' father, and come to terms with her own identity.

Reinventing oneself was all very well, but in the instant that she'd heard Samir describe Michael she'd known that if she had to choose between turning into a snooty rich bitch lookalike to stay with Samir or remaining her regular self and doing without him, she'd choose the latter. However much it hurt.

Still feeling a little shaky, and definitely not confident enough to go back upstairs, she veered off the jogging track and went to sit on a bench in one of the little artificial gardens next to the swimming pool.

Think, she told herself sternly. She'd already admitted to herself that somewhere along the line she'd fallen in love with Samir. Well, that couldn't be undone now—but what she *could* do was make sure Samir never figured it out. Which meant she'd either have to put on a front all the time, or leave as soon as she possibly could.

Her heart twisted within her at the thought of leaving, and she wondered if she wasn't jumping to conclusions. Maybe Samir just needed some time—there was nothing to say that he wouldn't decide to continue with their relationship. After all, he'd just told his mother that he hadn't made up his mind yet. Miserable as the hope was, it buoyed up her spirits temporarily, and she got up to go back to the flat.

Once Samir had finished his call, he headed back towards the tennis court, hoping to get a game in before dinner. He was lucky—one of his neighbours had just come to the court and was looking for a partner. The man was a lot older than Samir, but he was very fit, and the game was close.

'Great game,' he said after shaking Samir's hand. 'I thought I saw your wife around here a while back. Does she play as well?'

About to tell him that Melissa wasn't his wife, Samir held back and just said, 'No, she's never learnt.'

Mumbai was reasonably progressive, but he didn't want more people than necessary knowing that they weren't married. They would have some explaining to do if they actually *got* married, but that was something he was sure he could handle. He pulled himself up short before that particular train of thought could go any further—*could* they actually get married? Had he really been thinking that?

He took a deep breath. The conversation with his mother had unsettled him more than he wanted to admit. She'd always been unusually perceptive, and evidently she'd sensed that Melissa meant more to him than any of the girls he'd dated before. It wasn't something he'd allowed himself to think about much.

Melissa challenged him in ways no woman had before—sometimes making him question his whole approach to life and the way it should be lived. On the other hand, with her easygoing, undemanding ways, she was also incredibly easy to live with. And then there was the sex. Mind-blowing was an understatement, and he needed to be sure it wasn't clouding his judgement in other things.

When he got back to the flat Melissa was in the kitchen, looking very busy.

'Where's Kamala?' he asked.

'Kamala's taken the day off for Ganpati,' Melissa said. 'She told you a couple of days back.'

'We could have gone out,' Samir said, leaning against the doorjamb. 'We still can, actually. Let that stuff be and go and get ready.'

Melissa didn't look up from her chopping and marinating. 'It'll spoil,' she said. 'And I don't like eating out.'

Something was wrong—her voice sounded different and she still wasn't looking at him. 'We'll go to a Goan place,' he promised. 'Come on, Melly, you're starting a new job from Monday—you need to relax a little.'

'I find cooking relaxing,' she said.

Samir shrugged, beginning to feel annoyed. If she was upset about something, she'd have to come out and tell him what it was—he hated guessing games. 'Well, all right,' he said, turning away to go into the living room. 'Don't make anything very spicy, though.'

Melissa stared at the pan where she'd been carefully combining spices. She'd planned to make chicken *xacuti*, and there were six red chillies in the masala, waiting to be ground up into paste. Sighing, she turned the stove off.

'Let's go out,' she called after Samir. 'But not a Goan place, please—the ones in Mumbai are rubbish. Let's go to one of the places *you* like.'

'I was thinking I'd go to Goa for a couple of days,' she said over dinner. 'See my dad. I've left things to fester too long. I was looking at Brian and Cyrus and Darius today—they suddenly seemed so old…and Dad's the same age as Brian.'

'Are you sure?' Samir asked, his eyes warm and concerned. 'Last time you met Michael you came back looking an absolute wreck.'

'I've spoken to him since then,' Melissa said. 'I overreacted, I think, that time I met him. They didn't want Dad to know I was in town because he would have been upset I didn't go and see him.' With a flash of her normal spirit, she added, 'Though unless they thought I'd grown telepathic I don't know how they expected me to figure that one out.'

Samir smiled at that, but still came back to the topic once they were home. 'Should I come with you?' he asked. 'If you think your dad will be upset if he knows we're living together I can stay out of the picture, but at least you'll know I'm nearby if you need me.'

'I think I'll be okay,' she said. 'And it's something I need to do on my own. But thanks for offering to come with me. It…it means a lot.'

'Any time,' he said softly and leaned across to kiss her, his lips warm as they lingered on hers. It was a slow kiss, but it set her veins on fire, and she clung to him when he finally tried to draw away.

CHAPTER NINE

MELISSA TOOK THE overnight train to Goa—this time luckily the tickets were easy to get. Samir had tried to talk her into taking a flight, but her fear of flying was still too strong for her to attempt it alone.

Michael was at the station to meet her, and he put his arms around her and hugged her when she got off the train. 'It's good to see you, *men*,' he said. 'Dad's looking forward to seeing you too.'

Her father looked older and frailer than when she'd seen him last, but he was evidently very pleased to see her. She'd wondered how he'd manage the conversation about their two-year-long estrangement, but after a while she realised that he wasn't planning to talk about it at all. He seemed happier pretending that she'd been away for work.

'Brian told us about the new job,' he said. 'This boy you're with now—Samir—he's Hindu, isn't he?'

'Yes, Dadda,' Melissa said, heaving an inward sigh. Some things about her father hadn't changed. Presumably no one had told him that Samir and she were living together or he'd have disowned her all over again.

'If you get married will he convert?'

'I don't know,' Melissa said. 'I don't think we'll get married, Dadda. It's not that serious.'

Her father grunted. 'You be careful,' he said. 'Don't let people take advantage of you. And no need to tell them about what happened earlier.'

He sounded like a medieval father whose daughter had been raped by invaders, Melissa thought, torn between anger and amusement. Evidently he thought that her chances in the marriage market had dwindled after she'd run away with Josh.

The more time she spent with her family, the more the differences between her and Samir were underscored. She tried to imagine bringing Samir to her home. He'd probably be bored out of his wits—the conversation in their family revolved around food and films, mostly, and Samir wasn't interested in either. Then, of course, he'd have the option of hanging out with Michael and his mates from the band. Or with her father and the parish priest.

Her lips curved up in an involuntary smile. To be fair to Samir, he'd probably do both without even once indicating that he wasn't exactly enthralled by the company or the conversation. Only he'd be dying to get back to Mumbai, or at least to a more hip and happening part of Goa. Melissa's smile faded. In spite of the strong resistance her heart was putting up, her brain seemed to be coming up with more and more reasons why her relationship with Samir wasn't going to work.

The rest of her visit was peaceful enough, though it dragged a little—especially in the morning, when her nephew was in school and everyone else was busy in the restaurant preparing for the lunch crowd. She tried helping them, but she'd lost the rhythm of working in a large kitchen and, though no one said anything, she soon realised that she was in the way.

'I got this out of the safe for you,' her father said, handing her a small blue box on the day she was packing to leave.

Melissa opened the box to see a pair of heavy gold bangles that had belonged to her mother.

'Dadda…' she said, suddenly overcome. Her mother had worn those bangles to church every Sunday, and when she was very young Melissa had thought that her mother wouldn't be allowed in if she didn't wear them.

'She'd have wanted you to have them,' her father said heavily. 'I spoke to the Father, and he told me to look within my heart and think what my wife would have wanted me to do for my children. She would never have let you go away.'

So the parish priest had some sense after all, Melissa thought. No wonder Michael had tried to make her meet him when she was last in Goa.

'Thanks, Dadda,' she said.

She didn't have it in her heart to be resentful about the way he'd treated her. Parents were human as well, and who was to say he hadn't been right? Maybe if she'd listened to him and given Josh up she'd have been much happier. But she'd never have moved to Mumbai, and she wouldn't have met Samir... Probably by now she'd be married to Savio, who ran the neighbourhood grocery store and had always had a crush on her. She thought of Savio and his curly hair and sweaty hands and suppressed an involuntary shudder. Some things about the move to Mumbai had definitely worked out for the better.

'I'll come back and visit you soon,' she said, giving her father an awkward peck on his withered cheek. He nodded, and she picked up her bag and gave Justin and Cheryl a hug. 'I'll see you guys soon too,' she said.

When her train pulled into CST she automatically looked around for Samir, even though he'd told her he had an important meeting and wouldn't be able to come to the station. His driver was there, though, and she handed her bag to him and followed him out to the station car park.

Her phone rang as soon as she was in the car.

'Hey, there,' Samir said, and she felt her pulse quicken at the sound of his voice. 'Had a good trip?'

'The best,' she said. 'But I'm happy to be back.'

'Can't wait to see you,' he said, and his voice was a husky promise. 'I'm sorry I couldn't be there to pick you up, but there's a minor crisis at work. I'll get home as soon as I can this evening.'

'See you soon, then,' she murmured, mindful of the driver's being within earshot. 'Bye.'

It didn't take her long to unpack, but it took a lot longer to figure out where to put her stuff. The clothes were easy—they just went into the wardrobe in the master bedroom that Samir had cleared out for her. The problem was with the books and CDs she'd brought back from Goa with her.

There were quite a lot of them, she realised, staring at the heap on the bed. She'd left most of her stuff behind in Goa when she'd left with Josh, and she'd assumed her father had got rid of it when he'd done the whole disowning-his-only-daughter thing. As it turned out, though, Cheryl had carefully stored everything away, and in a fit of nostalgia that she was now regretting Melissa had carted almost all of it back to Mumbai.

She padded into the media room to examine the bookshelves there. Most of Samir's books were glossy hardcover editions of popular books on management and advertising. There were a few tomes on art, and the odd novel. Everything looked so perfect that Melissa wondered if the interior decorator had chosen the books as well as the bookshelves. There was no way her tattered collection of largely second-hand paperbacks would be welcome on those shelves. And there were no closed bookshelves or spare cupboards in the room—presumably they wouldn't have fitted in with the decor.

It was when she was investigating a small cupboard over the bar in the living room that she found the photo albums. The complete impersonality of Samir's flat had been bothering her for a while. There were no pictures or souvenirs, or anything that suggested a home rather than a hotel room. The albums had evidently been there for a while, and she dragged them off the shelf carefully and dusted them by clapping them together.

Sneezing as a cloud of dust rose up around her, she got off the chair she'd been standing on and inspected the albums. The older one had pictures of Samir as a young boy, standing solemnly with his parents on the shores of a lake, blowing out candles on a birthday cake almost as large as himself, and playing cricket with a bunch of equally small and solemn-looking friends.

The second album appeared to be exclusively filled with pictures from a single holiday. It was at least six or seven years old, and Samir looked young and carefree as he posed for the camera.

The pictures were mostly taken in Greece and Italy, and Samir seemed to have gone there with two other men his age. One of the men looked vaguely familiar, and after peering at the picture for a while Melissa realised that he was Vikas Kulkarni, the rather cynical-looking man she'd met first at Priyanka's party, and then at the art gallery.

'Searching for something?'

Samir's voice came from behind her, startling her so much that she almost dropped the album.

'Or generally snooping around?'

His tone was light, but there was an edge to his words that she couldn't fail to miss.

'Snooping around,' she said gaily, getting to her feet. 'Only you're not much of a Bluebeard, are you? This is the only cupboard I found with anything remotely interesting in it.'

'I'd forgotten I still had those,' Samir said, glancing at the albums. 'God, we were such a bunch of losers.' The photo he was looking at had the three men posing in completely ridiculous attitudes in front of the Parthenon.

'I don't know—I think it's a cute picture,' she said. 'You were pretty hot. In a boy-band kind of way.'

'As opposed to my current manly appearance?' he asked, raising his eyebrows as he took the albums from her and returned them to the shelf.

The tight expression had left his face, and he looked almost relaxed now. A four o'clock stubble darkened his jaw, and his shoulders looked even broader than usual in a well-cut formal shirt. He was right—there wasn't the merest hint of 'boy' in him now.

Feeling her mouth go dry with longing, Melissa hastily averted her gaze from his perfect shoulders and the even more perfect body attached to it.

'That's right—as opposed to your current old man appearance,' she said. 'Such a pity I missed out on your best years.'

'I'm not so upset about it,' he said gravely. 'You were probably in kindergarten then. I'd have been hauled up for child abuse.'

Melissa laughed, and looked curiously up at the albums before he shut the cupboard door.

'What about the girlfriend, then? Shivani... no, Shalini. How come she's not in any of the pictures?'

'Because she wasn't with us on the holiday, Einstein,' Samir said.

He seemed perfectly relaxed, and Melissa ventured a second question. 'So what was she like?'

Samir shrugged. 'Pretty. Bone-lazy. And as hard as nails.'

Melissa wrinkled her nose. 'Doesn't sound very appealing,' she said. 'Of course you could be prejudiced because she dumped you.'

'Very likely,' Samir said.

But he didn't seem to be really paying attention to what she was saying. Instead, he was looking at her, his dark brown eyes fixed on hers so intently that she blushed and fell silent.

'Did I happen to mention I missed you?' he asked finally, his voice low and scorching hot.

Trying to sound as casual as possible, she said, 'You did say something.'

His eyes glittered a little as he moved closer. 'And...?'

'And...well, of course it's natural, you getting a little lonely rattling around in this big old flat...' Her voice trailed off in an undignified squeak as a large, warm hand clasped her waist, and Samir swung her up into his arms.

He'd carried her into the bedroom when he stopped abruptly and said, 'Bloody hell, what happened to the bed?'

Melissa peeked over his shoulder and gave a gurgle of laughter. 'I got some of my old stuff back from Goa—I was looking for a place to put it, and that's why I opened the cupboard.'

But Samir was already striding purposefully towards the guest room. 'You can tell me all about it later,' he promised. 'Right now I've got more important things on my mind.'

Afterwards, Samir propped himself up on one elbow and gently traced a line down her arm, making her shiver with delight. One part of her brain was admonishing herself, though—it had been only a few minutes since they'd made love and here she was, going up in flames at his touch all over again. Shameless or what?

'I got you something,' he said, and she looked up in surprise.

He reached across and took a rectangular box out of the pocket of his discarded trousers.

'A watch,' she said, taking it out and smiling up at him. 'Thanks, Samir, it's lovely.'

And it was, with a delicate rose-gold strap and a mother-of-pearl dial studded with little diamonds. She wasn't sure if the diamonds were real, never having seen any close up. Goodness knew how much it had cost.

'I was thinking we should take a few days off and go on a holiday,' he said. 'Somewhere nearby, perhaps—Krabi or Koh Samui.'

'That's in Thailand.'

He smiled. 'Yes, but not the terribly touristy part. The beaches are great.'

Melissa thought hazily that she wouldn't care

if they *were* touristy. She'd never been outside India, really—a childhood holiday to Nepal *so* didn't count.

For a few seconds she daydreamed about having Samir all to herself for five days—maybe even a week.

Then reality sank in. 'I can't go,' she said. 'I'm starting a new job, remember? I can't saunter in and ask for leave the day I join.'

Samir shrugged. 'It's not such a big deal. Tell them you'd already made plans and you couldn't cancel. Anyway, there won't be much work right now while the Ganpati festival's on.'

She shook her head regretfully. The thought of a holiday with Samir was incredibly tempting, but she knew she couldn't mess round with Maya.

'I can't. And anyway, I'm phobic about flying, remember?'

'That won't be a problem if you're with me,' he said, so confidently that she had to smile.

'I still can't come.'

Samir shrugged. 'Maybe in a couple of

months, then,' he said, but it was clear that the idea had already lost some of its charm for him.

A couple of months.

She'd had a lot of time to think on the way back from Goa, but she'd still not made up her mind about staying or leaving. The one thing she was sure about was that she wasn't going to mould herself into a Stepford wife in order to make Samir propose to her. If needed, she'd do the opposite and make sure he understood exactly what he was getting into.

'What time are you getting back home tomorrow?' Samir asked, interrupting her thoughts. 'You'd better get in early—it's the last day of the festival and there'll be hordes of processions on the roads, taking the idols to immerse them in the sea.'

'I was planning to go and watch the *visarjan* at Marine Drive,' Melissa said. 'It's pretty amazing.'

Samir groaned. 'Mel, of all the crackpot ideas to have! D'you know how crowded it gets? Anything could happen!' He stopped short, realising that he sounded horribly like someone's fussy maiden aunt. 'It's not like you're even celebrating Ganpati Puja,' he continued after a brief pause. 'Why would you want to go for the *visarjan*?'

'Because it's interesting,' she told him firmly. Then she relented a little. 'There's a friend of mine who lives near Churchgate—we'll go to his place if it gets too bad.'

'Who's we?'

'Me and Neera and a couple of others. You can come along if you want.'

That last was clearly an afterthought, and Samir grimaced. 'No, thanks. I'll get home early and work from home for the second half of the day. You can take the car and driver.'

'I won't need them,' she said. 'We'll take a cab.'

'I'd feel safer if you had the car with you,' Samir said, frowning. Melissa came to him and gave him a conciliatory hug.

'Of course you would,' she said. 'But I don't need the car and I can take care of myself.'

'I know you can,' Samir said, pulling her closer. 'It's just that I like taking care of you as well.'

'Then come with me,' she whispered. 'Leave the car behind and mingle with the hoi polloi for once.'

The words were out of her mouth, said in her best temptress tones, before she knew what she was doing. Insisting on going for the *visarjan* was just another way of emphasising the differences between them; she hadn't *meant* to ask him to come along.

Samir hesitated only for a second before saying, 'All right, I will. In any case I won't be able to work if I'm worrying about what exactly you're up to.'

Damn, she hadn't expected him to actually agree. In spite of herself, though, Melissa felt a little thrill go through her. If he was willing to do something so out of character, just for her sake, surely that meant he cared? Then she gave herself a brisk mental shake and told herself not to be silly. If he cared he'd have told her. He wasn't exactly in *purdah*, was he?

'Where shall I meet you?' she asked. 'Don't bring the car anywhere near Marine Drive—the roads will be blocked for kilometres all around.'

'I don't think I'm really comfortable hanging around if Samir's going to be here,' Neera said. 'It's OK for you—he's your boyfriend and you don't work at Mendonca's any more. But he's my boss, and I'm sure he thinks we're mad, coming out to watch the *visarjan*.'

This was something that Melissa hadn't anticipated. Finally, she'd managed to convince Neera to come with her, but the rest of the gang from Mendonca's had dropped out. Worst of all, Samir had been right—the crowds were terrible and, unless you were actually with one of the *puja* committees, it was impossible to get anywhere near the part of the beach where the immersion was happening. There were cops everywhere, and without her usual gang around it was really no fun. The previous year, they'd accompanied one of the smaller Ganpatis actually into the sea, and it had been amazing. Being a bystander was not a patch on it.

'I think I'll head back,' Neera muttered. 'I've got to meet the rest of the guys, and I promised my mum I'd be home early.'

With her last supporter gone, Melissa acknowledged defeat. 'It was much better last year,' she said despondently.

Samir heroically refrained from saying *I told you so*—but her disappointment was contagious. Also, he suspected that it had been more fun the previous year because she had been with friends, and he knew he was responsible for their not being around this year.

'Maybe you should have just gone with your friends,' he said, putting the thought into words.

'Maybe,' Melissa agreed, giving him a rather lopsided smile. 'You wouldn't have had to slum it then.'

Samir sighed. 'That's not what I meant,' he said. 'If we're together, we can't live in a bubble, can we? It's just a question of adjusting a little.'

'But we're adjusting all the time,' she said slowly. 'You didn't want to come here, and you're hating every minute of it, only you're too polite to say it. And it's the same for me. I had to make an effort every single minute at that party at Priyanka's house. The only time we're together and happy is when we're in bed.'

'That's not a bad start, is it?' Samir said teasingly, but Melissa refused to smile.

'If we're together just for the sex—' she started to say, but Samir interrupted her.

'I'm in it for a lot more than the sex, Melissa,' he said. 'But I don't think this is the place to discuss it.'

It definitely wasn't—they were in one of the lanes leading off Marine Drive, but the music and drumbeats were as loud as if they were right on the beach with the Ganpatis and their worshippers. Also, some of the stragglers from the processions were giving them curious looks.

'Let's head back, then,' Melissa muttered.

Lost in thought, she stepped out of the lane right into a mass of people. Probably it was because she was walking in a direction opposite to the flow of people, or because she was still a little shaky after the conversation with Samir, but she felt herself lose her balance and trip. The procession kept moving—perhaps no one noticed her—and in an instant she found herself knocked into the path of a truck carrying a massive Ganesha.

There was time only for her to give one terrified scream before Samir's strong hands pulled her out of harm's way.

'Of all the careless…' He was very pale, and she noticed dispassionately that his hands were shaking as he half dragged, half carried her into a nearby doorway. 'Are you hurt?'

'No,' she said, leaning against a pillar to catch her breath. 'Just a little bruised.'

And more than a little shaken, though she didn't tell him that. For an instant, with the Ganpati looming above her, she'd thought she'd be crushed under it. So much for her enthusiasm about the *visarjan*—she'd never be able to see a clay idol again without thinking of the day she'd almost got herself killed.

'Thanks,' she said, smiling at him wanly. 'I don't think anyone else even noticed I'd fallen.'

He brushed her thanks away impatiently. 'Are you sure you're OK?' he demanded. 'You're as white as a sheet.'

'So are you,' she retorted without thinking, and he laughed grimly.

'You're back to normal, at least,' he said. 'God, Melissa, you really know how to keep things lively.'

A dozen confused retorts ran through her mind, but before she could say anything the skies opened up in a perfect torrent of rain. It was the tail-end of the monsoon season, and it had been cloudy all afternoon.

'Great,' Samir said with water streaming down his body. 'What a lovely end to the day.'

He was laughing, though—properly laughing this time—and after a few seconds Melissa joined in.

Samir held out his hand to her. 'Let's go

home,' he said. 'And don't you dare suggest walking back—we're taking a cab.'

'There's something about the rain and sex,' Melissa mused later on in the evening. 'Maybe it's all those old Bollywood movies with the leading ladies dancing in the rain in clingy white saris.'

'Or under waterfalls,' Samir said, lightly running his hand up her leg. 'Waterfalls were pretty big in those days.'

'Hmm…' Melissa gave in to the pleasurable sensations his hands were evoking and stretched like a cat, pressing her body even closer to his. 'Pity I don't own a chiffon sari.'

'Cotton *kurtas* can be pretty sexy too,' Samir said, smiling as he remembered what had happened in the afternoon.

They'd barely made it to the bed before collapsing in a tangled heap of wet limbs. Their damp clothes were still strewn around the living room and the passage that led to the bedroom—at some point they'd need to be picked up and put in the washing machine…

'All good, Mel?' he asked, and they both knew he wasn't talking just about right now.

Melissa gave a little sigh and pulled away, sitting up with a sheet tucked around her. 'We need to talk,' she said and prodded him with an elbow. 'Go and get some clothes on. It's very distracting, you sitting there without a stitch on.'

Ten minutes later they were sitting across from each other at the dining table, both fully clothed.

Melissa looked directly at Samir. 'It won't work,' she said.

Samir took a deep breath. He'd expected her to say something like that ever since their argument on Marine Drive.

'Why do you think that?' he asked. 'We've had a few ups and downs, but that's normal.'

'The ups and downs are normal,' she said. 'But that's not it. I don't fit into your world, and I don't think you want to fit into mine.'

'When you say you don't fit into my world…'

'It's all so artificial!' she said. 'You've got to be careful about what you say, and people are more bothered about how much money you make and what brands you wear than what kind of a person you are.'

'That's not true,' he said quietly. 'You just need to be yourself. But whenever we meet a friend of mine you seem to go out of your way to say something outrageous. Like what you said to Vikas at the art gallery. I'm not ashamed of the relationship we have. I'd like it to be a lot more than just sex, that's all.'

Put like that, it sounded very logical, and Melissa began to feel terribly guilty. Belatedly, it occurred to her that Samir had known these people for years, and the way she'd behaved reflected badly on him and his judgement.

Her shoulders sagged in defeat. 'It's not about your friends or mine, really,' she admitted. 'That can always be worked out. It's *us*. We have fun together, and the sex is great, but we don't really...*connect*. I still know hardly anything about you, and you don't seem particularly interested in knowing about me—though of course that doesn't stop me from babbling out my life's secrets at every opportunity.'

Realising that she'd lost the thread of what she'd wanted to say, and also that she wasn't sounding as calm and collected as she'd planned, she ground to a halt.

'I *am* interested in whatever you tell me,' Samir said quietly. 'I'm just not very good at expressing myself. And if there's anything you'd like to know about me, you only have to ask.'

'But that's just it—I *have* asked, and you always clam up!'

'Like what?' Samir's patience was wearing thin now. 'Ask me again. Ask me whatever you want!'

'What were you planning to give up your career to do?' she blurted out. OK, it wasn't the most important thing she needed to know, but it *had* been bothering her. He looked a little puzzled, and she clarified. 'You told me that Shalini split up with you because you wanted to go off to Europe and work on something that wasn't likely to pay much. What was it?'

His brow cleared. 'That…' he said. 'It was a bit of an impractical plan, really. I was crazy about cars—vintage cars especially—and the idea was to buy a bunch of old cars, work on them and set up a dealership. Also drive them in rallies and stuff like that.' He shrugged. 'What can I say? I was only twenty-two.'

'It doesn't sound that impractical,' she said. 'There's a museum like that in Goa, and I think they're doing pretty OK.'

Samir shrugged. 'Shalini didn't think so,' he said, and his mouth twisted for a few seconds in memory of that long-forgotten hurt. 'What else did you want to know?'

'You mentioned having to leave Kashmir. I can understand you not wanting to talk more about that,' she added hastily. 'But you don't talk about your parents much, or even your brother. At first I thought you weren't very close to them, but from what Priyanka said that's not true.'

Samir sighed. 'I'll tell you all about them,'

he said. 'Soon. I promise. Is that it? Or is there something else that's bothering you?'

There was, but it was very nebulous, and she certainly couldn't tell him about overhearing his side of his conversation with his mother. He was still looking at her, however, and finally she said, 'I keep getting the feeling that you're assessing me, somehow. As if you're trying to figure out whether I'm good enough for you or not.'

The last thing she'd expected was for him to go on the offensive, but he raised his eyebrows and said, 'And aren't *you* doing exactly that yourself? You've practically made a catalogue of everything that's wrong with me.'

'It's not the same thing—' she started to say.

He interrupted her ruthlessly. 'It's exactly the same thing,' he said. 'Neither one of us is perfect. But I still think we can make it work.'

He got up and came around the table to put his hands on her shoulders, bending down to nibble gently at her neck. In spite of herself, she squirmed against him with pleasure and he laughed softly.

'And if it doesn't work, at least the sex is great,' he said. 'That's a good reason to stay together, don't you think?'

The doubts crept back that night as she watched Samir sleep, his head pillowed on one arm, while the other was casually flung across her. She'd let him talk her into staying, but she wasn't at all sure that their relationship would last. Great sex was all very well, but they couldn't spend all their waking hours in bed. Other problems were waiting to happen.

She hadn't brought up their different religions because that was something that would matter only if they planned to get married. It bothered her, though. Samir was borderline atheist, and though she wasn't exceptionally devout herself, she *was* a believer. Also, he'd been raised Hindu, which meant his family mightn't take kindly to his marrying a Christian.

Samir stirred slightly in his sleep, his arm tightening possessively around her, and Melissa bent down and pressed a kiss onto his perfectly sculpted lips. Some things about him were perfect, even apart from his startling good looks and prowess in bed, and that was what made the decision so difficult.

In spite of her carefully guarded independence she'd come to depend on his quiet strength— she knew he'd never let her down if she needed him. And he had an irreverent streak in him that perfectly matched her own rather wacky sense of humour, and he always managed to tease her out of a bad mood. He was honest and straightforward, and a genuinely good person, and at the same time he was sizzling hot and pretty near irresistible to women. She would have had to have superwoman powers to stop herself from falling in love with him.

The breaking point came a few days later, when she figured out that Samir expected her to accompany him to a party that the Maximus top brass were holding on Friday.

'But I'm working,' she said. 'You said it yourself—it's a new job, and I can't take things easy.'

'Mel, the party starts at eight,' Samir said. 'Surely you'll be done by then?'

'I'll be done with my office work,' she said. 'But there's that short story Maya asked me to do for a magazine—that's due by Saturday morning.'

'Finish it today, then,' Samir said impatiently. 'How long is it supposed to be? One thousand words?'

'A little more than that,' Melissa said, and hesitated. 'I've actually finished it already. I just need a quiet evening to polish it up a little.'

Maya had lined up a book contract for her that would go through if the publisher liked the story, and she was on tenterhooks. She hadn't told Samir, though, instinctively feeling that he wouldn't understand. Or, worse, wouldn't think it important enough.

'Can't you do that between today and tomorrow?'

'It's…um…difficult to work when you're around,' she said.

The first two times she'd tried to sit down to

write he'd cajoled her into bed. After that she'd scheduled her writing for when he wasn't at home.

'I won't disturb you,' Samir said tightly. 'Get the work done and keep Friday free.'

Melissa stared at him, feeling very torn. The party evidently mattered to Samir, and though she didn't want to attend it in the least she'd have gone if not for the short story. The solution he was suggesting didn't work for her. She wanted to let the story be for two days and then come back to it on Friday. Right now she was finding it difficult to be objective—she might ruin it completely by over-editing it.

Samir picked up on her hesitation and said quietly, 'Right, I guess that means it's a no, then. All the best with your story.'

'You haven't even asked to read it,' she blurted out.

'This is the first time you've mentioned it since you told me that you'd been asked to write it,' Samir said. 'If you want me to read it I'm more than happy to.'

Melissa didn't say anything, and Samir went out of the room before he could say anything he'd later regret. He'd come to respect Melissa's individuality, but today's behaviour seemed plain selfish by any standards.

His lips curved up in a mirthless grin. Most of his earlier girlfriends would have jumped at the opportunity to be seen with him in public. Melissa, however, seemed to see it as an imposition.

It was on impulse that he picked up his phone and dialled a number that he hadn't accessed for a while now.

After a largely silent dinner, Melissa said quietly, 'I'll come with you.' She'd thought the whole thing over, and decided that she was being rather immature. Unless she explained to Samir why her writing was so important to her she couldn't expect him to understand—he wasn't clairvoyant. And if the party was important, she owed it to him to go. Whether she enjoyed it or not, he was providing her with a lifestyle that was light-years beyond her means, and so far she'd done very little to show her appreciation.

Samir looked up. He was already regretting the hasty phone call he'd made, but what was done couldn't be undone. And maybe it would help bring Melissa to her senses.

The brusqueness of his tone as he replied was a measure of how uncomfortable he was with the situation, but Melissa didn't know him well enough to realise it. 'It's all right. I don't need you to come,' was what he said.

'But I want to,' Melissa said, hoping her nose wouldn't grow longer. As whoppers went, that was the biggest one to come out of her mouth in a while. 'I've figured out how to manage the work thing.'

'I wish you'd told me earlier,' Samir said. 'The thing is, it's kind of mandatory to bring a partner along, and once you said no I had to invite someone else. My secretary's already put her name down on the invitee list.'

He knew Melissa would assume it was an ex-girlfriend he'd invited, and in a sense it was true. Rita and he had dated for a while, but then she'd met Vikas Kulkarni and fallen head over heels for him. Their marriage had broken up recently, and as in most divorces friends had been forced to take sides. He'd been slotted into the Vikas camp. Privately, he thought that Rita and Vikas would get back together, and part of the reason he'd asked her to the party was so he'd get an opportunity to talk some sense into her.

Melissa's eyes were wide with disbelief, but her voice was as light as any practised socialite's when she said, 'Oh, OK. I assume you didn't find it too difficult to find a replacement, then?' Only a slight quiver in her lips betrayed how upset she was.

For a few seconds Samir was tempted to call Rita and tell her the party was off. She'd understand, and it would get rid of the betrayed look in Melissa's big brown eyes. Then suddenly anger kicked in. She had no business looking at him like a wounded deer, given that it was *her* unreasonableness that had landed them in this situation in the first place.

'No, it wasn't difficult at all,' he said, and his voice was as cold as ice. 'Replacements are always available.' It was probably his evil genius that prompted him to add, 'Maybe that's something you should keep in mind.'

There was a long pause, and then Melissa said quietly, 'I've been thinking about it for a while, actually.'

For a few moments she thought Samir would melt and take her into his arms, and she could go back to pretending that everything was great. But he didn't say anything and he didn't move towards her.

Quite suddenly she couldn't take it any more. Getting to her feet, she said, 'I'd better go and get writing. See you around.'

CHAPTER TEN

'I'M SO SORRY.' The matron didn't look sorry in the least. 'You told us you were moving out for good. Your room was allotted to someone else the very next day. And the waiting list has some twenty names in it—it'll be at least a year before you can get a room again.'

Melissa put her name down anyway, but her shoulders slumped as she walked out. The working women's hostel wasn't ideal, but it was cheap, clean and safe, and it had been her home for two years. The other options were significantly less appealing—either she could find someone who took in paying guests, or she could move to the suburbs, where rents were lower. Leaving Samir's flat had been an impulse decision—she hadn't really thought out where she would go. Right now she was occupying the spare room in Liz and Brian's flat, but she couldn't stay there indefinitely.

As she was leaving the hostel one of the girls she knew slightly caught up with her. 'No luck with Matron?' she asked sympathetically.

Melissa shook her head. 'She's got a waiting list as long as her arm.'

'One of my friends has found a place, and she's looking for someone to share it with her,' the girl said. 'Do you want to check it out? You'd get along well, I think.'

It was one of those things that clicked immediately. The studio flat was tiny, but new and clean, and there was a direct bus from right in front of the building to Melissa's office. And Rohini, the girl she would be sharing the flat with, was plump and cheerful, with a wacky sense of humour.

'I was supposed to be sharing this place with my boyfriend,' Rohini confided as she locked the flat door behind her. 'Then he decided to go back to his wife—which was a bit of a surprise, seeing as I didn't know he was married in the first place. And there I was, stuck with a lease that had only my name on it and a rent I couldn't afford. How about you? Any ex-boyfriends or stalkers I should know about?'

Melissa shook her head, smiling slightly. 'Couple of ex-boyfriends, but they're not likely to bother you. One of them isn't even in the country.'

Rohini put her head to one side, looking a lot like an inquisitive bird. 'And the other one?'

The other one. For a second, the memory of Samir's tense, angry face swam in front of her eyes and she felt a physical pain in the region of her heart.

'The other one wasn't important,' she said, smiling slightly at Rohini. 'So, when can I move in?'

'Today, if you like,' Rohini said. 'Or tomorrow. You decide. The quicker you start paying your share of the rent the better, as far as I'm concerned.'

And the quicker Melissa moved out of Liz and

Brian's flat the better. They'd been wonderful, but she couldn't impose on them any longer.

Liz was a little tearful when she moved out, but Brian looked relieved—he'd missed his peaceful routine and having Liz's full attention.

Between her job and her writing, Melissa managed to stay so busy that she hardly had time to think. The nights were toughest, and she lay awake for hours while Rohini slept like a baby. In the mornings she pretended that she'd had a proper night's sleep, but she had a feeling she wasn't fooling Rohini one bit. The thought that she'd made a colossal mistake was eating away at her, and it took all her will-power not to answer Samir's calls or try to contact him herself.

It still hurt when she thought back to the morning she'd left Samir. She'd waited in the bathroom the morning after their row until she'd heard the front door shut behind him. Then she'd scrubbed her face, come out of the bathroom, and made several valiant attempts to write him a note.

An hour later she'd been out of tissues, and had had nothing to show for it other than a few torn up sheets of paper. So much for her skills as a copywriter, she'd thought wryly. Perhaps she should tell Maya Kumar that she'd been hired on false pretences. Giving up on the note, she'd put all her things into the two suitcases she'd brought with her and, carefully pulling the door shut behind her, she'd taken a cab to Liz and Brian's apartment.

On the surface, there had been no real reason to leave—when Liz had asked her what had happened, she'd just told her that things weren't working out rather than explain that she'd refused to go to a party with him, and he'd taken someone else. End of story. And, of course, he'd told her that replacements were easy to find— probably true, given that it had hardly taken him ten minutes to find another companion. But that had been all. Any other woman would have laughed it off and done her best to charm him back into a good mood.

It was the depth of hurt she'd felt that had surprised her. If she'd felt that bad about him going to a simple party without her, she'd have been devastated if he'd actually left her for someone else. And the way things had been going it had become very likely he'd leave her—sooner if not later. Leaving of her own accord had seemed to be the only option.

It was only after she'd moved out that doubt began to gnaw at her. Pride had kept her from answering his calls or calling him herself, but she couldn't help wondering if she'd completely misjudged the situation. Maybe he'd been upset with her because he cared? But if he cared he wouldn't have given up so easily—he'd have come after her, not just dialled her number a few times.

'You OK?'

Rohini was standing just behind her and looking so ludicrously concerned that Melissa had to laugh.

'Yes, of course,' she said, though it was an effort plastering a cheerful smile on her face. 'Let's go—we'll miss the movie otherwise.'

It was a mercy Rohini was such good company without being inquisitive, Melissa thought later, as she struggled to follow the plot of the movie. It would have been torture getting through the past couple of weeks without her.

For an instant she thought she saw a glimpse of Samir in the audience, and her heart-rate tripled. Then the man turned, and she realised she'd been tricked by a chance resemblance.

'Brian, I just need to know where she lives now.'

'Maybe if you ask her...?' Brian said, peering up at Samir hopefully.

Samir shook his head in exasperation. 'She refuses to answer my calls,' he said. 'It's been three weeks.'

Brian shook his head. 'If she's not taking your calls, I can't tell you, can I? And when I was your age, if my girlfriend had walked out on me I wouldn't have waited three weeks before trying to figure out where she was.'

Samir passed a hand over his face. 'I had to go to Delhi,' he said briefly. 'My father wasn't well.'

His father had suffered a mild heart attack the day after Melissa left, and Samir had had to leave for Delhi at about an hour's notice. Even now his mother had agreed to his returning to Mumbai only because his younger brother had come over from the US to be with his parents.

The past few weeks had been tough—while the heart attack itself hadn't been serious, the doctors had discovered a lot of other health issues, and his father had been hospitalised for over a week. Keeping his distraught mother calm had been an uphill task, and all the while he hadn't been able to stop thinking about Melissa.

For the first few days he'd tried calling her almost every day, and messaging her when she didn't take his calls. He hadn't mentioned his dad's illness because that would have been playing a sympathy card. She'd replied to his texts, saying briefly that she was sorry she'd walked out without telling him but she'd made up her mind—she wasn't coming back.

'I can pass on a message or a letter if you'd like,' Brian offered.

Samir shook his head. 'No, I'll figure it out. Thanks anyway, Brian.'

'Did you read the story Melissa wrote for that magazine?'

Samir nodded. He'd picked up a copy of the magazine when his father had been in the hospital. It was very simply written and incredibly moving without being in the least soppy—about a young girl who'd lost her mother when she was ten, and then spent the next seven years of her life searching for her in other people. Her laugh, the curve of her neck, the fall of her hair… Then finally, when she was seventeen, she'd looked into the mirror and found her mother staring back at her. Not normally a very sensitive person, Samir had found his eyes had been damp by the time he'd finished reading it.

'It was brilliant,' he said. 'She's got real talent.'

He sat with the older man for a while, talking about advertising and the recent changes at Mendonca's.

It was when he was getting up to leave that Brian cleared his throat and said, 'She thinks you don't care about her.'

Samir stared down at him in surprise, and Brian continued hurriedly.

'She didn't say anything to me—I couldn't help overhearing when she was speaking to Liz. She said that it made more sense to leave of her own accord before you threw her out.' At Samir's thunderous expression, Brian said, 'Well, that's what she said. I was pretty sure she was barking up the wrong tree, but I don't like interfering in these things.'

Before he threw her out. Why would she think he'd do anything of the sort?

Samir's hands clenched into fists as he left Brian's flat. Clearly he'd made an even bigger hash of things than he'd thought he had. He thought back to what he'd said the night before Melissa left. He'd made that ill-advised crack about replacements, but he didn't think just that would have made her think she needed to leave. And he'd fully intended to apologise, but when he'd got back home from work the next day she was gone.

He'd had to leave for Delhi almost immediately afterwards, and it had only been after several attempts to contact Melissa that he'd admitted to himself how much he cared about her. It had taken another week for him to realise that she'd carved her way into his heart—if this wasn't love, he didn't know what was. He thought about her practically every minute of the day, and her absence was like a physical ache.

And when he'd come home the house had seemed so empty without her that he'd had a second's mad impulse to go and find her and not come back until she agreed to come home with him.

It had been stupid, not telling Melissa that he loved her and wanted to marry her, but he hadn't known it himself. Thinking back, the only conclusion he could come to was that he'd been appallingly selfish. He'd known from the day he'd met Melissa that she was special, but he hadn't ever let her know. Instead, he'd bided his time, trying to figure out if their relationship would work, throwing her into one situation after another to see if she'd fit into his social circle.

No wonder she'd felt he didn't value her enough, and finally that he didn't deserve her.

Picking up his cell phone, he dialled her number yet again, not thinking for a minute that she'd answer.

He almost dropped his phone in surprise when her soft voice said, 'Hello?'

'Hi, Melissa, it's Samir,' he said stupidly.

'Yes, I know, your name comes up on the screen.' Her voice was cool and controlled, but her knees were shaking so badly that she had to sit down.

'You doing OK?' he asked.

His voice managed to be low and gentle and sexy all at the same time, and Melissa blinked back sudden tears. She'd not realised quite how much she missed him until she heard him speak.

'All good,' she said. 'I'm sorry I didn't take your calls earlier—I've been a bit…um…confused, I guess.'

'I need to meet you,' he said. 'Please, Melissa.' She hesitated, and he said urgently, 'Just for a short while. We can't leave things like this, sweetheart—we need to talk, and not over the phone.'

He was right—they *did* need to talk. Only she wasn't sure if she could face him without breaking down and telling him exactly how unhappy she'd been since she'd walked out on him almost a month back.

'We can meet,' she said slowly. 'But I don't want to come to your place. After work some day would be best.'

'Today? I'll pick you up around six.'

Melissa had a deadline for a shampoo ad, and another for an ad for super-crunchy peanut butter. In the state of mind she was right now she'd probably write about crunchy hair and extra-lather peanut butter…

Sighing in defeat, she said, 'OK, then. Do you know where it is?'

'I'll find out,' he said. Before he rang off he added, 'Mel? I've really missed you.'

Me too, she thought as she put the phone down. *Me too.*

She was staring vacantly into her screen when Maya walked by.

'Searching for inspiration?' she asked drily.

Melissa sat up in alarm. Maya was a wonderful person to work with most of the time, but the one thing you absolutely could *not* do was slack off at work. In the short time Melissa had worked with her she'd seen grown men turn into weak-kneed jellyfish when Maya raised her perfectly plucked eyebrows at them.

'No, I was just…' she started to say, but Maya wasn't listening.

Leaning over, she slid the briefing document for the shampoo ad out from where it was currently serving as a coaster under Melissa's bottle-green coffee mug.

'Concentrate,' she said. 'If you're PMSing, pop some medication, and if it's a boyfriend he's probably not worth it.'

At six-twenty, after having dashed off two lyrical pages on strawberry-scented shampoo and one more on the health benefits of peanut butter, she stood on the pavement outside her office. Maya was wrong, she thought. Samir was totally worth it. But she could have done with some of Maya's inner strength, she thought as she hungrily watched Samir cross the road to come to her—she was in imminent danger of turning into a helpless little puddle of need.

When he was finally standing in front of her she had to take a deep breath so that she didn't show him quite how affected she was by his proximity. He looked good enough to eat, she thought, drinking in the sight of him in an open-necked denim shirt and perfectly cut beige chinos. He was thinner, his sculpted cheekbones a little more prominent than they had been, and there was a haggard look in his eyes that she wanted to kiss away.

'Hey,' he said softly, touching her cheek. 'It's so good to see you.'

A whiff of his woody cologne teased at her nostrils, and the temptation to lean closer was immense. Once again she felt deeply thankful that she'd suggested meeting in a public place.

'It's good to see you too,' she said as graciously as she could, doing her damnedest to channel Maya Kumar. Strong, smiling, with a core of steel. She gave a yelp of alarm and jumped backwards as he bent his head to brush his lips lightly against her cheek. Okay, now she was channelling Chihuahua, not Maya, and passersby were giving her funny looks.

'Should we find some place we can sit down?' he asked, his lips curving up in his trademark half devilish, half little-boy way.

'There's a small restaurant a little way down the road,' she said, a little breathless. 'Not swanky, but we can talk there.'

She turned and started walking towards it,

hoping she didn't trip and fall flat on her face in her agitation. The worst part was not knowing *why* he was here—perhaps all he wanted to do was have a civilised conversation before they called it quits on their relationship. Then again, maybe not. The way he'd looked at her suggested that he wanted to do a lot more than just talk—his dark eyes had smouldered into hers in true romantic hero style. Though this time she'd been too rattled to tease him about it. Instead, she'd lowered her head and done her best to memorise the cracks in the pavement.

Samir fell into an easy stride by her side. 'Congratulations on the story,' he said. 'I just finished reading it. I don't know what to say, Melissa—it was brilliant. I had no idea you could write so well.'

It was ridiculous to feel so pleased. She knew that. Trying to sound as nonchalant as possible, she said, 'Thanks. All credit to Maya, though— she put me in touch with the magazine. Left to myself, I'd have decided the story wasn't good enough to send anywhere.'

'I'm glad you met Maya, then,' he said. 'Though I still haven't forgiven her for stealing you away from Maximus.'

'From Mendonca's,' she corrected. 'We're here—the red door is the place we need to go. It serves the best Indian-Chinese food in the city.'

They stepped into the unassuming little restaurant and found an empty table in a corner.

Samir waited while the server plonked two menus in front of them and wandered off, and then asked bluntly, 'Why did you leave? Was it because I invited someone else to that party?'

Melissa bit her lip. 'No,' she said. 'That wasn't it. I just thought it wasn't working any more.'

'Why?' he asked, leaning forward. 'We might have had a few issues, but we could have worked those out. What was so bad that you had to leave?'

'Sir—order?'

Samir looked up in exasperation, but the little waiter refused to budge. The restaurant managed to keep its prices low by keeping the turnover high—one thing it absolutely didn't encourage was people dawdling around, occupying tables and staring into each other's eyes without ordering anything.

'Ask for either the chilli chicken or the Idli Manchurian,' Melissa prompted. 'And a diet soda for me.'

'Idli Manchurian?' he said in disbelief. 'What is that?' As was usual with Melissa, the conversation was slipping off into a direction he hadn't planned.

Melissa gave him a lopsided grin. 'Idlis rice cake, sliced up, dipped in cornflour, fried and tossed in Manchurian gravy.'

'I wasn't really asking for the recipe.'

'Oh, it tastes great,' she said. 'Though there's enough garlic in it to ward off an invading army of vampires.'

Samir shuddered. 'We'll have the chilli chicken,' he told the waiter. 'And two cans of soda.'

He gave Melissa a wry look once the boy had zipped off into the kitchen. 'This isn't exactly the right place for an uninterrupted conversation, is it?'

No, that's why I chose it, Melissa thought. 'I'm sorry,' she said out loud, more Aunty Liz than Maya Kumar this time. 'But there are no fancy places around here. We'll have to make do with this.'

Samir was about to reply when the boy waiter returned with a large bottle of soda and two glasses which, going by the state of his sleeves, he had just rinsed in the sink.

'Soda,' he announced proudly, and Samir sighed.

'Thank you,' he said, pushing the bottle across to Melissa.

'So I was asking.'

'Chilli chicken dry or with gravy?' his nemesis asked, popping out of the kitchen.

'Dry,' Melissa called out, suppressing an involuntary giggle as Samir sank his head into his hands in exasperation.

'Spicy or medium spicy?' the boy asked.

Samir gave him a look, and he promptly vanished back into the kitchen, saying as he went, 'Medium spicy better for you, I think.'

'You know what? Let's cut to the chase,' Samir said. 'I've been a self-centred pig and I've probably ruined my chances with you, but I just need you to answer one question.'

Melissa looked at him, her eyes wide.

'Is there any way you would consider marrying me?'

Her answering gasp was loud enough to make diners at the other end of the restaurant turn around to stare at them.

'Of all the…' She was sputtering in anger now, but Samir was leaning back, his dark eyes dancing with amusement.

'I'll take that as a yes,' he said. 'If it was an unequivocal no you'd have been much nicer to me. Come on—let's go.'

He was on his feet already, and before she knew what was happening she was standing next to him, still clutching her bottle of soda.

'We won't be needing that chilli chicken after all,' Samir informed the diminutive waiter as he put a five-hundred-rupee note into his hand. 'Madam has some really important work to do.'

The boy flushed with pleasure as he pocketed the money, and Samir swept her out of the restaurant.

'But…where are we going?' Melissa asked, thoroughly confused now.

'Some place where I can propose to you properly,' Samir said. They were already in his car, and he turned to look at her, his eyes warm with suppressed desire. 'And some place where I can kiss you the way I want to.'

'Hang on,' Melissa said.

Samir turning all masterful on her was an incredible turn-on, but she needed to know what was happening.

'A month back you weren't sure you wanted to be with me. Then I walked out, and you suddenly want to marry me?'

'I always wanted to marry you,' he said, starting the car and turning onto the road. 'I just wasn't sure it was the sensible thing to do.'

'What's changed then?' she asked.

Samir shrugged. 'Nothing major,' he said. 'Except that I've figured out I can't live without you.'

The words were said in such a matter-of-fact way that for a second she thought he was being flippant. Then she saw that his hands had tightened on the steering wheel so hard that his knuckles had turned white. It must have taken considerable effort for him to say that, she realised, especially since he was normally so restrained. And he hadn't said the words, but the implication that he was in love with her was pretty loud and clear—people didn't say they couldn't live without you if they were only mildly fond of you.

And, come to think of it, she was finding it pretty hard to live without him as well.

'Let's go to your flat,' she said, her voice sure and steady for the first time that evening.

She was having a bit of an epiphany, she realised. She'd got it wrong all along—fooled by Samir's apparent coolness into thinking that he didn't care for her. But now that she thought back she realised that right from the beginning he'd been the one trying to make the relationship work, while she'd fought her feelings at every step. They'd been at cross purposes all along.

They were both silent till they were inside the door—then Samir pushed it shut behind them and took her into his arms, the raw hunger on his lips matched by the passion on hers.

It was a while before he released her, saying raggedly as he pushed a hand through his hair, 'God, I love you so much. I was crazy to think this was just about the sex—I want to spend the rest of my life with you, Mel.'

'So do I,' Melissa said, putting up a hand to caress his face and stealing a quick kiss before she went on. 'Spend the rest of my life with *you*, I mean, not myself.'

The rest of what she'd meant to say was lost as he crushed her lips under his in a kiss that managed to be hot and hungry and wildly passionate all at the same time. A little moan escaped Melissa's lips as she finally abandoned herself to the tide of sensation that was sweeping over them both.

Much later, he said softly, 'I was all kinds of fool to say what I did about replacements. I should have known better—I was just so worked up about you refusing to come with me that I let my mouth run away with me.'

Melissa gave the offending mouth a consoling kiss. 'I wasn't thinking straight either,' she said. 'I'd overheard you talking to your mum a few days before that, and I thought you felt I wasn't good enough for you. You even said you weren't in love with me.'

Samir frowned. 'When did I say that?'

'The day your mother called on the home phone and I spoke to her. You called her back from the car park—I'd gone for a jog, and I couldn't help hearing you. You said you needed to sort things out with me...'

His brow cleared. 'That was a long while back,' he said. 'I already knew I didn't want to let you go, but I hadn't got around to figuring out that I was in love with you. We hadn't discussed marriage. And my mother tends to get a little ahead of the situation at times. When things didn't work out with Shalini she was perhaps even more upset than I was.'

Seeing that Melissa looked puzzled, he went on.

'She lost a lot of her family in a militant strike around the time we left Kashmir. So it's her dream to have a large family again—both her sons married, lots of grandchildren, the works. If she'd known things were even remotely serious she'd have had us kidnapped and taken to the nearest registry office before we could change our minds. But I promise you—the second I get a ring on your finger, she'll be the first person I'll tell.' He bent his head and planted a little row of kisses on her shoulder. 'And you'll need to speak to your dad as well.'

'He'll want us to have a church wedding,' she said. 'And bring up our kids as good Catholics.'

'If the priest doesn't mind performing the ceremony I don't mind,' Samir said. 'As for the kids—they can grow up and decide what they want to be.'

'Very permissive,' Melissa said teasingly, but a great load was off her shoulders.

Samir wasn't done yet, though.

'There was another thing I wanted to tell you,' he said. 'I mayn't have come across as being very supportive of your career or your writing. Maybe I was a little jealous of the time you were spending away from me. But I'll back you every step of the way from now on. You've got real talent, and you deserve every possible bit of support I can give you.'

Melissa nestled a little closer to him. 'Even if I bunk off your incredibly boring office dos to write?' she asked.

'Even if you do that,' he said. 'I'll probably bunk off them as well and stay home to watch you.' His expression turned serious, and he cupped her face in his hands, tipping it up so that he could look directly into her eyes.

'I love you,' he said. 'Corny as it may sound, I'll love you till the day I die.'

'In some situations corny is good,' she said, and she met his gaze squarely. 'I love you too, Samir. And I'd love to marry you, and grow old and cranky with you, and have several kids.'

The last bit came out all muffled against his lips, and Melissa gave up the attempt to outline the path she wanted the rest of their lives to take. She loved him, and he loved her back, and right now that was all that mattered.

EPILOGUE

THE WEDDING WAS in Goa, in a little church near Melissa's childhood home. They'd had a big Hindu wedding first in Delhi, followed by a register office ceremony, but to Melissa exchanging their vows in the church she'd gone to for all her growing up years was the most important of the series of ceremonies.

'You look beautiful,' Cheryl said, carefully adjusting Melissa's veil. 'I'm so glad you decided to wear your mamma's wedding sari.'

The sari was made of lovely white brocade, and Melissa had insisted on wearing it instead of an elaborate wedding gown of the kind popular in the current generation. A single perfect strand of pearls gleamed at her throat—they were one of Bina Razdan's many gifts to her brand-new daughter-in-law. With her silky hair piled up in a chignon, Melissa looked like a graceful young queen.

'I wish Mamma could have been here,' Melissa said softly as her sister-in-law gave the veil a final tweak and stepped back to admire her handiwork.

Cheryl bent down and gave her a hug. 'I'm sure she can see you,' she said. 'And that she thoroughly approves of that gorgeous man you're marrying.'

Melissa's father was waiting for her at the door of the church, and as they slowly walked down the aisle Melissa's eyes sought out Samir's. He looked incredibly handsome in his dark formal suit, and his eyes lit up as she reached him. Cheryl was right, Melissa thought with a sudden rush of pride. He *was* gorgeous—and, better still, he was all hers.

'Have I told you yet how much I love you?' he whispered as they took their places in front of the parish priest.

'Many times,' Melissa whispered back. 'But

I have short-term memory issues—you'll need to keep telling me every so often.'

'Shh…' Melissa's father said, smiling at them fondly.

He'd taken an abrupt liking to Samir, and that had helped heal things further between him and Melissa. It was as if the whole episode with Josh and the two years after that had never happened at all.

The ceremony was performed by the young parish priest who'd encouraged Melissa's father to reach out to her. In his early thirties, and almost as good-looking as the bridegroom, he was attracting languishing stares from the younger female members of the congregation—his attention, however, was solely focussed on the couple in front of him.

When he said, 'You may now kiss the bride,' there was a mixture of sighs and gasps from the audience.

Melissa suspected that if they hadn't been in a place of worship people would have whistled and stamped their feet. Then Samir's lips came down on hers, and for a few seconds she forgot about audience reaction as the world closed in to accommodate just the two of them.

When they broke away a minute later her cheeks were flushed and her heart-rate twice what it had been when she'd entered the church. 'Not fair,' she muttered under her breath, and Samir smiled at her, his expression so openly and radiantly happy that she felt her heart miss a beat.

'I love you,' he said once again, and though he kept his voice low it was strong enough to be heard by the people in the front pew. 'She has short-term memory issues,' he explained to the priest, who had paused to grin broadly at them. 'I need to keep reminding her.'

'Welcome to the family,' Samir's father said, beaming as he raised a toast to them at the lunch that followed the wedding.

His mother gave them a lovely smile, and Melissa thought for the nth time since she'd met Samir's parents that she'd been so completely off the mark when she'd thought that they wouldn't accept her. Ever since she'd met them they'd gone out of their way to make her feel she was part of the family. So much so that she'd had to be careful not to offend them when she'd insisted on doing the preparations for the wedding herself and refused the ridiculously expensive gifts they'd tried to thrust on her.

'Congratulations,' Vikas Kulkarni said. 'Could I have the honour?'

Michael had arranged the music, and the members of his band had now loosened their ties and were playing popular Goan dance numbers.

'Can you dance?' Melissa asked suspiciously.

In her experience most non-Goan men hadn't mastered the art of dancing with the opposite sex—they either flung their arms around enthusiastically and stamped on their partner's toes or stood stock-still and tapped their feet to the music, presumably expecting their partners to gyrate around them Bollywood style. Neera was currently dodging a partner of the second category and giggling over a drink with one of Samir's Maximus colleagues.

'My ex-wife forced me to go through an entire year of Latin ballroom dancing classes,' Vikas said as he expertly swung her onto the dance floor. 'Good music, by the way, Melissa. Michael's done an amazing job.'

'Thanks,' Melissa said. 'Though I think a couple of Samir's relatives are absolutely scandalised by my band party family.'

Vikas glanced over at the relatives in question. 'Oh, I wouldn't bother about them, if I were you,' he said dismissively. 'Sour-faced bunch of prunes. Just remember their faces and snub them royally if they volunteer to be godparents to your babies. Samir's parents are in love with you, and so are his friends. Even his brother's bowled over.'

Melissa laughed, hoping he was right. Bina had confided to Melissa that she'd always had a secret yen for a church wedding herself, and she was thrilled to be part of one. Right now she was being whirled around the dance floor by one of Melissa's cousins, while Samir's father looked on with an indulgent smile. He'd completely recovered from the heart attack, but he still needed to take things slowly—Bina was trying to convince him to retire and hand over the business to Samir's brother to run.

Melissa's eyes met Samir's, and for a second she forgot to move, forcing Vikas to steer her abruptly out of the way of a couple doing the *bhangra* to a peppy Konkani number.

'I can see I've lost you.' Vikas sighed in her ear, and she blushed vividly. 'But before you rush off to your loving husband could you be a darling and introduce me to that lovely flat-mate of yours?'

Sadly, Vikas and Rita hadn't reconciled, in spite of Samir's best efforts—Rita was now seeing someone else, and Vikas was revelling in his new-found bachelor status. Melissa took him across to Rohini, whose eyes promptly lit up. There were clearly some serious sparks going on there, and Melissa left them to get on with it as she headed back to Samir.

'I've been thinking for a while, and I've now made up my mind,' Melissa announced later as they got into the car to leave for their honeymoon.

Samir looked at her in mock alarm. 'Statements like that make me very nervous,' he said. 'What exactly have you decided, Melly?'

'Today is quite definitely the happiest day of my life,' she said. 'I was trying to choose between today and the day you asked me to marry you. But today is better.'

'It is,' Samir said, brushing his hand gently against her collarbone and making her shiver with longing. 'But I'd like to think that we have even better days ahead of us.'

'Fabulous honeymoon sex,' she said, wrinkling her brow as she pretended to concentrate very hard. 'Setting up house together.'

'Our first child,' Samir supplied.

'Second child.'

'Third… Actually, no, our first child's graduation day.'

'His wedding.'

'Grandkids.'

Melissa began to laugh. 'We seem to have it all mapped out,' she said. 'Our own version of happily-ever-after.'

'Everything might not turn out exactly the way we think it will,' Samir said, turning to smile his trademark heart-stopping smile. 'But the happily-ever-after bit—that's non-negotiable.'

'Completely,' she agreed. 'Though I *would* like the bit about fabulous honeymoon sex to turn out the way I've imagined it.'

And it did.

* * * * *